SAHARA

Piercing the Thatch Ceiling

A/Prof. MIMMIE CLAUDINE NGUM CHI WATTS, Ph.D.

IEM PRESS

PO Box 831001, Richardson, TX 75080

A Subsidiary of IEM APPROACH

Published by A/Prof. Mimmie Claudine Ngum Chi Watts Ph.D. First Published 25th of May, 2018 Melbourne, Australia.

IEM PRESS (PO Box 831001, Richardson, TX 75080) functions only as a book publisher. The ultimate design, content, editorial accuracy, and views expressed or implied in this work are those of the author. This book is a novel, but for the names of some places, all characters and people are fictional. 56051 words.

ISBN 13: 978-1-947662-88-9

Library of Congress Catalog Card Number: 2020908675

TABLE OF CONTENTS

.

DEDICATION

This book is dedicated to:

My husband, Dr Christopher Michael Watts;

My children, Sherry–Rose, Tracy-Kate and Michael- Christopher;

My parents Pa Christopher Chi Nkcam (RIP) and to my Ma Veronica Shuri Chi; and to my Family.

Part one

CHAPTER 1

Sahara in Cloud Class

Sahara looked like a statuette, tall with smooth silky ebony skin. She was medium built with a generous backside. Her arched brows framed her face. Sahara's smile was unforgettable; though she rarely smiled these days let alone with strangers. When she did smile, you could feel the radiance from her hazel bronzed eyes pierce through your heart. She was habitually described as the ideal beauty. She was smart too. Sahara, was fun to be with though could be serious too. A girl from an affluent family, a qualified accountant, she became a skilled, refugee. Just when she thought all was lost, her story began all over again.

Sahara looked at her boarding pass; she smiled and turned left into business class on the AirTrain Class A440. The AirTrain Class A440 was a hybrid of a rocket, the Airbus and the high-speed train, sleek and packed with technology. As Sahara took her seat, the gentleman next to her turned and greeted her. They smiled at each other, shook hands then took their respective seats in the comfort of Cloud One. Shortly after, a voice came over the pager; as the screen monitors changed to 'Announcement' at the same time. The voice was soft but resolved.

'Good afternoon and welcome aboard AirTrain A440, flight AT008 from Adika to Melbourne. My name is Captain Amira Songe and my co-captain is Ashumi Maryana Hassan. We are pleased that you have chosen to fly with us today and we will be taking you to Melbourne. The weather conditions look fine and we expect a smooth flight in general. Welcome on board again, our all-female crew will look after you. Sit back, relax and enjoy the flight.'

The announcement came to an end and Sahara nodded while speaking at the same time, 'this is good.'

As Sahara relaxed and smiled the look on the face of the gentleman next to her seemed otherwise.

'Are you okay? Do you have a fear of flying sir?' Sahara asked gently with a concerned look on her face.

'Not a fear of flying; did I hear we have an all-female crew?' I have never seen a woman fly a plane, not been in one that the captain was female let alone an AirTrain like this one, this is the most advanced of planes.'

Sahara responded with a devious smile.

'Is that why your face turned pale just then? Welcome on board and I think you should relax; we are in 2018 where women can have an equal seat around the table. These women just took their seats at that AirTrain table.' Sahara responded with a devious smile.

The flight attendant interrupted the conversation asking them both what they desired as refreshments. They requested some Champagne and freshly roasted macadamia nuts, that were promptly served.

As they relaxed in their seats Sahara's mind moved away from the worries of the gentleman next to her to the last visit of Afrika, Mumene and Veronique's in Melbourne some years ago and their upcoming one.

Sahara recalled that she had only returned to Melbourne from trying to trace her parents' disappearance a few days before their last visit. These four have been close from childhood. She had longed for them and she had hoped they felt same about her. Back then she flew B Economy. Today she could recline, lay flat and sleep during this flight. *When Afrika, Mumene and Veronique, arrive after such a flight I won't be in the state they found me that time. Hopefully, I won't be too tired.* Sahara smiled as her thoughts returned to her childhood.

Sahara and her three 'friends' had grown up together, remaining close, despite living across different continents today, but for Afrika. All aspired to lead in their respective fields. They were prepared to work towards it.

Today Sahara was in Cloud One on the most expensive AirTrain. As Sahara sipped Champagne, she not only ruminated about her three friends, she thought of Johnny, her husband, with their two sets of twin sons and daughters. Sahara thought about her beloved Ahbotta, the mother-in- law with the intelligent mind, sharp tongue, and witty sense of humour that came with the gentleness of a dove. *How could Ahbotta be all this?* Sahara wondered.

The flight was smooth as expected. A few hours into the flight, Sahara turned to her fellow passenger, the gentleman. He appeared to be, in his early mid-sixties, seemed good- natured and cordial, quite the gentleman in fact. They discussed various topics during the flight but there was no repeat of 'all female crew,' though other topics on women, men and work dominated their conversation.

After the plane landed, the same voice they had heard at the beginning of the flight announced.

'Welcome to Melbourne where the local time is 11:30am. The current temperature is thirty degrees Celsius. It has been an absolute pleasure flying with you and we hope you enjoy your stay in Melbourne. For those transiting, we wish you a safe journey to your next destination. Thank you for flying with us and we look forward to welcoming you again aboard the AirTrain with our all-female crew.'

At that point the voice disappeared. As the AirTrain taxied on the tarmac, Sahara stretched her legs and arms. She so wanted to stand, but the seatbelt sign was still on. Sahara yawned, murmured something to herself then turned and looked at her new friend, the gentleman in the seat next to hers.

'Nice flight and we landed without any of those bumps.

Any thoughts on the 'all female crew?' Sahara asked.

'They flew us over 40,000ft and crossed the Indian ocean. Who could have imagined this in my Mother's Day? I think every time I travel, I shall ask for an all-female crew. That's my preferred travel crew option now.'

Sahara was surprised by the response. She opened her eyes and mouth.

'I did not need to convince you after all. You experienced it for yourself, women taking a seat. A new convert to our faith, sir?'

'I shall now consider everything you told me, my child, on the flight about women and their capabilities. If I had a choice at the start of this flight, I would have bailed out. I was not too sure they could fly an AirTrain like this one. I had my doubts, but when you are belted, and on the runway, there isn't much you can do. I felt helpless for the first time in many years. I must confess, I quietly prayed for my mother to look down on me wherever she is.'

Sahara smiled then replied.

'You prayed for your mother and not your father? Weren't you worried about being in the AirTrain captained and co-captained by women, after all? Prayed for your mother's protection, instead.'

'My child, the pleasure is mine and I hope you stay in touch. I know how to find you.'

'Bye sir.' Sahara said as they shook hands firmly and walked towards the exit to collect their luggage. The gentleman smiled back at her. He, like Sahara was also the CEO of an ASX listed company. That is now but it was not always like that for Sahara.

As Sahara waited to collect her luggage, she turned on her phone. It beeped enthusiastically as the messages loaded. Sahara had 56 new messages and 20 missed calls in total. *I have been away only for five days.* She did not read the messages; instead she placed the phone back in her *Chique* handbag while her mind went straight to her family. Sahara had flashbacks from the last visit by Mumene, Afrika and

Sahara. *They will be here within days again. We should have a good time.* Sahara thought to herself.

The driver was waiting outside for Sahara, as always, on time and reliable. As they exchanged greetings, Sahara offered him the gift she had for him from this last trip. His daughter and Sahara knew each other from their school days, so he was more than a driver; he was a friend's father and therefore, family.

As they rode home, Sahara shared the story about the gentleman who had sat next to her on the AirTrain. He laughed, then responded, 'if only he knew your story Sahara. If you have his contact details, ensure you make time in coming months to share a coffee with him. He sounds like he needs your smart mind on these matters, Sahara.'

'I think he needs your wisdom more, Mahmud. You have six daughters and a wife, that's seven women in your home. I know the girls are now grown up and all doing their own thing, but there was a time they were all home with you.'

'Yeah, I was worried when my wife gave birth to the first daughter, then a second, a third... I thought God had punished me. So, we tried the fourth, fifth and then the sixth time. My wife cried every day, because you know, the community gossip. My mother wanted me to take in another wife. My brother had two wives already, as you can understand, I had my brother's support. My mother put pressure on me. She wanted a grandson from his son. She even stopped speaking to my wife. She blamed my wife for bearing only daughters. My mother cursed her. I loved both women but I had to decide. I even had to convince my own wife, I am fine with the daughters and swore I will not take another wife. That was her greatest fear. Today when I look back, I am glad I did not listen to my mother, Sahara. My first two daughters you know have post graduate degrees in law and accounting. The second two have engineering and the last two are now completing medicine. The first two have struggled to find work, but I know they will.'

'So, you have the job list for the African family covered: Lawyer, Engineer and Doctor.'

At that point, Sahara and her driver laughed out aloud. They understand that expression quite deeply. If you were not and had not studied any of those or proceeded to complete a doctorate or a Ph.D., then you were option four, a failure in the eyes of the family. That was the fourth job option. The parents always wanted the first three options. Did their children feel the same?

During the fifty minutes ride, they discussed Afrika, Mumene and Veronique's upcoming visit. He would pick them up from the airport at the respective times.

'I will share their Itinerary with you tomorrow.' Sahara told her driver.

CHAPTER 2

Ahbotta and the old ways

Sahara recalled the last visit by Afrika from the Northern Territory, while Mumene and Veronique arrived from Europe. That was some three years ago. It had been a special time, as always with these *cousin friends* whenever they are together. Over the three weeks they stayed up until the early hours of the morning almost every night. They reminisced about their childhoods, shared their childhood dreams and reflected on their lives then and now. Then reality struck when it was close to their departure day.

Sahara woke up several times that night anxious about her extended family and the people she grew up with.

Over breakfast, Sahara's eyes welled and to her surprise she cried. In torrents, tears gushed down her cheeks. Her nose ran. She rubbed her eyes but the tears wouldn't stop. By now her face was 'blue.'

Mumene stood up and pulled Sahara towards herself.

Sobbing and mumbling Sahara buried her face in Mumene's chest.

'I'll miss you Mumene. Afrika, I love you. Veronique, oh my heart, when will I see you again? Oh, dears.'

'Sahara we aren't leaving yet! We have another day with you, girl.' Veronique reminded her.

'I know. But it is not enough. A year together will not be enough to catch up on everything. You know it is more than the chats and gossip. It's the connection; having people I trust, whom I love and have shared my life with. You know me and I know you. That is what I miss, the person, that person within each one of you. The people and the strength I have whenever we are together. That is why I cry.' Sahara altered these words as she pushed back the tears.

'I love you Sahara, and you Afrika and you Veronique,' said Mumene.

'I'll miss this gang, my #AfricanGang; you know the gang is here. We are together here in Melbourne, with me!' Sahara said as she wiped her eyes with a beautiful blue and pink handkerchief Ahbotta gave her.

'Sahara, we are still here and we hear you,' whispered Afrika.

'Oh, poor thing, the emotions, missing us already, we are still here at least for now' Veronique said as she extended her arms and held Sahara tight, and the others joined them in turn. They hugged each other for a minute. The emotions among these four women were deep and strong; it reflected the bond that existed between them.

As Sahara sat there, her mind wondered. *As children we dreamt of life in a faraway land…? We never considered loneliness as part of the price we would pay.*

'Sahara, do you recall we dreamt of the beautiful land, the people and all the nice things about abroad? The adults failed to share the lack of social networks, loss of friendships and disconnection from all we knew. The focus was always on what we shall 'gain', the money we shall make, lifestyle, what we could buy with the money we made and not what we shall lose; a far greater price to pay. Some people lost their minds. A friend did and her neighbour's children are school dropouts; imagine that in first world countries, none of the older ones have qualifications. Their mother can't raise her voice or speak to them sternly or firmly. The children threaten her with 'we shall call the police if you scream at us.' She goes out to work, cooks and cleans. They were good kids but something 'disconnected' somewhere some time. The children feel they have no identity; *'we have no one we can go and spend a weekend with, no relatives, no family, no real friend. But we have money, a lot of it too.'* The parents think the rules are too relaxed. The children blame the parents, the parents blame each other, the fathers say it's the mothers, the mothers state it is the fathers, both say it's the system and the system blame them too. So, who is responsible for the mess? Who is to blame the children, the parents or the system?' Veronique reflected and questioned.

'The reality is we have a problem, be it identity or opportunity; but we need to look beyond what is here. A form of cultural connection may be our best way forward. Do these children know their own history? Do you know your history? Do you know who you really are? What's your lineage? Children and parents regardless of where they were born need to know the answers to these questions. If they can't then there is a missing connection somewhere.' Afrika replied.

As they sat in the beautifully decorated room and pondered these matters, Ahbotta glided in quietly. This was very unlike Ahbotta to slip into a room silently, though Ahbotta could be sensitive to people's emotions at times, this was one of those times. Sahara's friends were leaving in coming days and Ahbotta knew how this would affect Sahara.

The aroma of boiled coffee began to fill the air from the other room.

'Now who was to make the coffee for you ladies? It's boiled over and overflowing.' Ahbotta said.

'This ebony was looking after the pot?' Smiled Mumene with her eyes fixed on Afrika.

Afrika jumped out of her seat, 'OMG, that was me, we all got caught up in the moment Ahbotta. Your daughter-in- law would not stop crying this morning and we are not even going yet. Not for another two days,' as she made her way swiftly into the kitchen.

Ahbotta followed Afrika into the kitchen.

'Never mind, I turned it off. I'll get the coffee for you people. Go back and join the others. Go and sit with your 'sisters'.' Ahbotta shooed Afrika out of the kitchen. Afrika obliged. There was no need arguing with Ahbotta, the matriarch. Ahbotta was gentle but had a firm and determined nature. She had lived and overcame a lot of challenges in her lifetime and those things shaped her.

Like a bunch of flowers, Afrika bundled herself onto the large settee with the others already there. It was as if they were reliving their childhood.

Sahara still distressed cleared her throat.

'Afrika, you should have sat on the sofa. We are so squashed here. Who's, going to move?' asked Mumene.

Sahara interrupted before it could go any further.

'Okay ladies, I'm sorry, just could not bear to think this was almost over.'

'Sahara, we all feel the same, so do not apologise. Let me get you a glass of water,' replied Mumene.

'Mumene, I'm bringing the water, let her rest. You people should sit and talk. Young women these days never sit down to rest. You have become like men, work, work, work.'

Ahbotta's voice could be heard from the kitchen only a few meters away.

'Oh, Ahbotta, won't you rest?' retorted Sahara

'What have I been doing that I need to rest? You people want me to just sit here, eat and get fat? Look at my belly?' Ahbotta said pointing as her stomach. 'I'm not pregnant, no, no baby. This is food. Bad food.'

'Okay, Ahbotta enough said. Thank you for my water.'

'That's so my child. I'm bringing the coffee soon,' Ahbotta said as she turned and walked back towards the kitchen. The aroma of the coffee could be smelled from where the ladies sat and it was stronger by the minute. The four ladies sat impatiently waiting for their mid-morning serve of coffee. Tears gone but not forgotten, the atmosphere seemed normal again.

'Yes Afrika, what were you saying before I started crying?' Sahara broke the silence with a forced twinkle in her voice to cover her embarrassment that she had cried so much in front of these friends. The others chuckled and Mumene almost choked over her coffee. She coughed into Sahara's half-tearing, half-smiling face.

'Oh no, Mumene, I have coffee all over my face and my dress. Stop laughing, was I not crying?' Sahara said with a more serious tone in her voice but the little tweak around her mouth and eyes said otherwise.

'Mumene, Mumene, your cup of coffee is all over me too,' screamed Veronique.

'Oops, sorry,' said Mumene It all happened in a splash.

Veronique and Afrika laughed loudly as they all joined in to help clean the mess they caused.

Ahbotta was there in an instant, walking stick under her left armpit and two large green tea towels in her right hand. She threw the cloths at her daughter-in-law and Mumene. They knew exactly what they must do. The look on Ahbotta's face said it all. That was not uncommon with the mothers, looks were enough to make a child 'sit up' or change behaviour without any words altered. Such looks, often from the side of the eyes and followed by a deep sigh for further effect were intended to make the child feel uncomfortable. They understood the message. It is a skill that the mothers used if they found themselves in situations that words could not deal with or words could not be uttered. That was the look from Ahbotta but this time she added words to it.

'Sahara, use that to clean your 'sister'.' Grasping her stick with the other hand, Ahbotta turned to the others.

'Now, all of you stand up and go sit at that table, there and I'll bring you some more coffee. Mumene, go and change that dress before your fiancé comes. Get something that if you spill coffee on it will not show, but that we can 'see you' since you can't help missing your mouth.'

The ladies obeyed without question. Mumene giggled, Ahbotta returned to the kitchen and within ten minutes was back with another tray containing four fresh cups of coffee brewed from the raw coffee beans Ahbotta had roasted and pounded earlier.

'Thank you Ahbotta, what will I do without you my mother?' Sahara said with a smile.

'My child, you brought me God's fruits'.

'Ahbotta this coffee is just the way my grandma used to make it. It smells good too,' Afrika said as she sipped her coffee slowly savouring every sip.

Ahbotta took her usual seat in the main room, next to the fireplace. As she made herself comfortable in the chair, she turned her attention to Sahara and her friends for the third time during their three-week stay. Ahbotta coughed, then began:

'I see you ladies had a cry this morning, you laughed, messed up yourselves and messed my settee but happy. That is what I think coffee time should be. When I was a child, coffee time was when women sat around the fire and shared stories. Before machines could do the work, it was back breaking for our mothers and fathers, still is for many of our rural farmers. As children, we helped our mothers and fathers too. It was a tedious process. Our mothers would roast the beans from the previous year's harvest. They sometimes had coffee beans that were years old. Post-harvest season the beans were fermented, washed then dried. Then the skin had to be peeled off. It was after such preparation that often went for weeks or sometimes longer that the beans were ready to be roasted to bring them to a state ready for consumption. That last stage involved roasting the beans; pounding them in a mortar using a pestle and then boiling the finished product for consumption. We had special mortars and pestles just for coffee. Every house owned at least one of those. In every kitchen it was a utensil that nobody could do without.

When our mothers sat together to drink coffee, the children played with each other outdoors. As kids, we were free. We wondered about the bushes, went and spent hours by the river. We loved going in groups as it meant you had others to play with. There were always lots of children around. My mother had seven, her sister had eight and my mother's co-wife had seven too. The children played outside while the mothers discussed women's business among themselves. That's how I learnt to be a mother. As you got older you cared for the younger siblings, nieces and stepsiblings. We did not have the word 'step'; we were just called siblings and my stepmother was simply my other mother. The word 'step' takes away that connection and separates people. It was and is still not in our language. The women shared their personal stories with each other. They shared stories about what their husbands were up to, the newborn babies in the community, who fathered what baby to what lady, who the next brides to be were, who had died and so it went.

Their stories developed to a maze, it was community gossip during coffee time. These informal women gatherings provided a safe place for the women to let go harmlessly. When I look back my children, coffee time was the 'strength' for those women, our mothers. Back then women could sit and be mothers and their husbands went hunting; the husbands brought the catch at the end of each day. The women cared for the home, cooked and cleaned. Back then, women were women, they mothered; and men were men, they fathered. The children fetched water and wood, they were allowed to be 'silly' and be children. They ran around barefoot. I do not recall ever seeing two of my younger brothers with shoes around the compound. Though I must say there was one that hated a bath or even a wash. It was always a fight with my mother when she had to put water on his back. He is now a multimillionaire and when I talk about it he laughs. But that was what being a child was like to us. I am not sure if I could say that in some countries today, but I am Ahbotta, that was the way of our people.

That's why we love the *Akirteh* women's group that I go to here. At Akirteh, we can share stories about our lives, our successes and struggles. What is said at Akirteh remains there. When I saw you four women in here Sahara crying, laughing, choking and drinking coffee at the same time, I thought for the first time in the last three weeks that you were actually being women. You reminded me of the ways of our people. That it is normal to sit together, laugh, cry and share your burden with each other. When you are together don't talk about the next shopping trips and what clothes who wore. My mother forbade me speaking about such. She always reminded me how bad it was to compete or look at what the other woman had or did not have. My mother said 'you do not know what happens under their roof because the proverb goes; *the thatch covers every problem in the house.*' That meant there were lots of secrets within family and they were often untold. The thing is, the mothers gave us such advice but I wonder if they respected it when they were among themselves. The women discussed the women's business among themselves; the *Takapbengs*, they are called. My mother seemed poor and so was my father but today when I look back, they were actually happier. They worked hard, very hard, but they also had others to share their day and burden with. They had days of the weeks assigned just for cleaning and resting. They had many community festivals, which they attended almost weekly. Communities mourned those who died young but celebrated the lives of those who lived to old age. HIV hardened our hearts and dried the tears from our tear ducts. It was almost becoming normal to not cry when a child died, because you turned around and saw another mother who had lost two or even three children. They were often left alone with the grandchildren. While my people used to cry and wail for the young after they died, HIV / AIDS back then broke us such that we could be broken no more. *What does not kill you my children strengthens you.* That bad illness strengthened us because some of us survived. But I lament that there are still people who do not believe that this disease exists. They think it is witchcraft when someone in their community dies. They now call it cancer or slow poison or deny it outright. I thank God that in my lifetime we now have treatment. That if people do the right thing, take their medicines correctly, they can lead a 'normal' healthy life. I know this because I lost many people my children and...'

As she talked, Ahbotta got tears in her eyes; past experiences resurfaced. She cleared her throat, sighed and continued.

'What was I saying again? Argh, my mind wandered... that sickness is a bad sickness; it did not care whether you were rich or poor, man or woman, young or old, famous or not famous. It touched everyone in my community. It strengthened us and made our mothers marry us young. But while it was easy to determine and protect the girl's virginity through control, as they would say, the same level of control and scrutiny didn't apply to our brothers. They were free, and many of them fooled about. It was very hard for us, the girls. Now it is harder for you young women today. How are you going to control your children in today's world? The children can watch everything on those small screens. Even if they sit there with you, they could be somewhere else. Back then, if the mother was not around, the eyes of the aunts and other mothers around were on you. There was no hiding anywhere, anytime.

My children take time from the life of money and look after you. Stop being busy! Watch your children grow! They remember the time you spend with them not the things you accumulate. Sit down like this every week and have coffee, laugh and cry! Even if you're alone, do it.' At that point Ahbotta stood up and just as she was about to walk back into the kitchen, Mumene started to speak.

'Ahbotta, times have changed. This is 2018, women go to school, they work, they earn money and they decide what they want. There is childcare, they do care about the children. The children learn and have other children to play with. Ahbotta do you know some husbands even choose to stay at home, look after the children, care for the home so their wives can work?'

With a gentle but firm clap, eyes wide open and fixed on Mumene Ahbotta spoke again.

'My daughter, let me tell you something, you do not know what you are talking about, hmmm… what you are missing. You take your child leave them with another woman so that you can go to work? Is caring for the child at home not work? Or is that because no one comes to give you money at the end of the month for looking after the children, cleaning the house and cooking that you don't call it work? It's house duties, interior affairs. Believe me, I feel sorry for you mothers today! Work, work, work! A father, looking after the children? Mothers away? If my grandmother returned to this earth she will not recognise it my children. In Muka where I come from there is a proverb that goes '*let it rain where the house once stood.*' Ahbotta mumbled to herself, sighed, then stood up and walked away.

Ahbotta's stories never failed to astonish Sahara and the grandchildren even when they've heard them before. They were the folk tales of their heritage that she would share with the children. Now Sahara's friends could understand why she was so fond of Ahbotta. Ahbotta told more than stories. She shared wisdom. After all, '*what an old woman could see sitting down, a young girl could not see standing up.*' Stories were Ahbotta's way of opening up to the younger generations. The ways and wisdom of the ancestors were recorded orally and passed down from generation to generation through stories with the hope that they could somehow be recorded and passed down through further generations.

Sahara, Mumene, Veronique and Afrika had just listened to one of her many stories from her early days, but she had gone on to discuss HIV/AIDS. Sahara knew Ahbotta was health-literate on pregnancy and motherhood issues, but not on HIV/AIDS. Ahbotta's experiences, so different to theirs, actually provided insights they could learn from; how those who saw their way as the ideal way could miss so much. It demonstrated that the younger generation could discover, admire and even embrace the old ways.

After listening to Ahbotta, the four ladies stared at each other in silence. They allowed Ahbotta's words of wisdom to sink deeply into them. *'Let it rain where the house once stood.'*

Mumene with her mouth slightly open, looked confused as she stared at the garden. She thought about her fiancé and his family. His father, he had told her, was a qualified electrician and a 'stay home dad' who had reportedly raised him. His mother was a successful serial entrepreneur; she earned a handsome income for the family business. Mumene's fiancé was open to the role of 'stay home dad' should they marry and have a family of their own someday. *Did Ahbotta just change all that?* She wondered.

While Afrika, Mumene, Sahara and Veronique looked perplexed, they were not so surprised with Ahbotta's view. Veronique contemplated her own mother's world, that of her generation and of children born and yet to come. *We know our own mothers' worlds and understand the social and cultural norms.*

Their early lives were shaped by those same norms and structures. Their children could not say the same. Their understanding of their people's ways was learned from books or shared in a foreign land.

They were not expected to live like their forbears. But how can one live a culture only through the stories of a few people rather than through a whole community? How could you show something you never had? How could you be part of something that you did not have the opportunity to be a part of?

'This is a different world', Veronique exclaimed as she stood up and stretched her legs. They swung back to their previous conversation prior to Ahbotta's intervention.

'Mumene, didn't you hear Ahbotta? Wear something coffee spill proof! You can be so stubborn! Sahara teased.

'Aren't we all stubborn, loud and uncontrollable?' Have you not been told that before? Leave me alone! Do you want me to dress as if I was a widow? I shall go and wear a black *'Cabagondo',*' retorted Mumene.

Cabagondo is a long flowing traditional dress, loose from the chest down and flows down to the ankles. Generous amounts of fabric can be used to make one *'Cabagondo'.* Fitting around the chest from just below the sternum, it flows generously down to the ankles. Anyone with a full figure or who is traditionally built looks respectable in one of those.

'Wear something that is good enough to cover you up, but interesting enough for him,' Afrika interjected.

The four were enjoying their coffee time and for once seemed to be in the world of their mothers and grandmothers. Ahbotta was always a good host and refilled their cups; they were having the third round of coffee, always the best part of the brew.

When coffee is freshly brewed in the traditional way, it is drunk in three rounds, each going for about half an hour. The first round is the *'salutation'*, the second, *the unwind* and the third and final round, the best of the rounds is called *the gratitude*. Coffee time could go for an hour and a half, or more. It's enough time to share stories and resolve any differences.

Now that they were immersed in *the unwind round,* Sahara and the others sipped their coffees. They discussed work, reflected about their respective roles, and shared their disappointments and the lack of recognition and the contribution they made. Sahara was demoralised about the little recognition of Afrika's skills.

The conversation was suddenly interrupted; it was a buzzing noise. A bee flew into the room through one of the widows, it buzzed around the room. It went straight towards Mumene, then towards Afrika. They both screamed almost at the same time. Ahbotta heard the screams and hurried into the room. She thought, *not another coffee spill.*

'It's a bee Ahbotta, it may sting someone; It's actually quite considerable. Veronique remarked.

Ahbotta smiled in contentment as she observed the bee buzz around the room for a moment. She then spoke.

'It looks like a queen bee too, do not shoo it away. A buzzing bee brings good news. But the queen, it's bigger news.' Ahbotta's voice was soft but firm as she uttered the words. She was more surprised by the startled looks on the lady's faces; it surprised her they were scared. Ahbotta was astonished they could be terrified instead of being exultant after such a 'visit'.

'Oh, Ahbotta what news yet again?' Veronique said as she eluded the bee that came straight at her face.

'Is one of you pregnant?' Ahbotta asked as she fixed her gaze upon each one of the ladies in turn.

Mumene with a firm clap, then held firmly clasped turned to Ahbotta, looking straight into her eyes and shaking her head from side to side went, 'Eh Ahbotta, maybe it is Sahara, she will give Ahbotta more of God's 'fruits.''

Sahara on hearing her name, leapt to her feet.

'I've done my bit, one, two, three four,' Sahara touched her finger tips as she counted off the numbers, then in a deep voice she added, 'DONE; industrial unit closed, for good. Mumene maybe it's you? Or maybe it's Afrika? But the bee went straight for Mumene.' Sahara said as she turned and fixed her eyes on Mumene who appeared anxious.

'She is the one, affianced,' Veronique added.

Ahbotta beamed with pride as she strolled back to the kitchen. *She thought to herself, another grandchild maybe.*

CHAPTER 3

Childhood, dreams and aspirations

As they sipped their coffees and ate *Chinchin,* they recalled making *Chinchin* as kids with flour, eggs, milk, butter, sugar, water, nutmeg, salt. Making *Chinchin* was an all-day chore for the family's children and their friends. It served as family-bonding activity with roles divided by ability. The older siblings did the more taxing activities such as precisely measuring and mixing the dough, while the younger ones cut and made patterns out of the dough, which was deep-fried in hot oil. An adult or someone in his or her mid-late teens had this task. It was the riskiest part of the whole process; it involved frying in hot oil, sometimes on an open fireplace. Consuming the end product masked all the effort and labour that went to making the *Chinchin.* While it looked simple; it was a complex undertaking that required skills and several people to do various tasks simultaneously. It was often served at parties, social and family gatherings; Chinchin making has now become a commercial activity. Sahara lamented this after she asked her 'nieces' to prepare Chinchin; their response was to simply get it from the local supplier. They were in their mid-teens and this was an unfamiliar task to them.

For Sahara, *Chinchin* making was always a reminder of family and festivities. For students in boarding schools, this was what they took with them; Chinchin helped sustain them as a favourite snack while they were away at school often for several months. *Unfortunately, the art of Chinchin making like other art forms and initiatives was quickly dissipating. Some of our younger ones will never experience the thrill of making something as simple as Chinchin. The whole process showed us the rewards of bonding and socialising.*

They enjoyed the Chinchin as a snack with their midmorning coffee. It would last a couple of months in an airtight container. As they enjoyed this product from the previous week's labour, it evoked memories and childhood aspirations, as they settled in the *relax*, the last round of their coffee.

'Veronique, do you recall when we were would make *Chinchin* at my parent's place, how we discussed our lives abroad? How we shall work in those blue-chip firms, the diamonds, smart cars? We dreamt, did we not?' Sahara asked.

'Afrika, that Audi, what make was it again? Within months of getting a new job, what happened?' Mumene asked with a twist in her left eye, lips pursed.

'First job my ... Could that even buy me a ten-year-old Corolla after six months? I had to eat and pay BILLS my dear.' Afrika responded.

'Mine was that job at that Hill Firm; I am still waiting for it ladies,' added Veronique.

'It was as if these jobs were there and we were just going to walk in and grab them. How ignorant! We thought the world was what we were told. Did all those people lie to us?' Sahara mumbled.

'I know, right? I wished someone had told me that to have all these qualifications was no guarantee for a good job here, yep, no guarantee indeed.' Veronique added.

'Seriously correct! Could I ever imagine that my father's child will one day work in a chicken factory plucking feathers of dead chicken?' spouted Mumene.

'Hmm, Mumene; you are talking plucking chicken feathers; I cleaned toilets! Ah, toilets' Sahara said as she moved her head vigorously from side to side; clapped her hands. 'Eh, with all what is in this head' she added, pointing to her forehead.

The four ladies were deep in conversation and did not even notice that Ahbotta had slipped into the room.

'Have you people finished that coffee? You have one more round to go' Ahbotta reminded them.

'Thank you Ahbotta, we planned a trip to the shopping mall today. Have to finish the last day, spend those dollars and cents before heading back to our Euros and Pounds.' Mumene responded with a smile on her face. Mumene then motioned the others to stand up so they could leave. But they knew they had to finish the last round of the coffee. It was customary and respectful, especially from a grandmother like Ahbotta. They were quick and within no time, the ladies were on their way to the city mall. It was almost the last day before departures to their various destinations.

'I wonder when we shall do this next.' Afrika said.

'Well as often as we want and can afford.' Mumene said.

'What do you mean by often?' asked Veronique.

'Every twelve months, or...?' Said Sahara looking at the others with questioning eyes.

'Okay, twelve months!' They responded in a chorus. Sahara looked at all of them and firmly; 'is that affordable? I mean flights and everything else? Every twelve months is quite an ask. Remember we are still waiting for those JOBS.' On that note Veronique sighed. It was a laborious sigh as if to say, *you are right; nothing has actually turned out the way we thought.*

Then with a sudden change of mind as if to say, *does it matter?* Veronique led them to the empty table at the corner of the room that the attendant showed them. The space had beautiful paintings all over the walls. They were evenly arranged. It must have taken a skilled decorator and person to do the job. It looked neat. The spaces between the paintings appeared even. The room looked exquisite and Mumene turned to Sahara.

'Just what I like Sahara.'

'I know that's why I brought you here. It's beautiful here', she responded.

'I wish we could do this all the time, I mean come here often, see each other often.' Veronique added.

'We used to see each other every day.' Said Afrika.

'True,' Mumene added.

The attendant returned, leaned over and he recognised Sahara. They exchanged greetings.

Sahara introduced her friends to the attendant, a handsome young man who waited to supplement his fees at law school.

'I like him, he will do for you Afrika.' Mumene whispered to Afrika as the attendant took their orders.

'Not sure about his status, but will check it out, only it's not happening today.'

'Why?' asked Afrika

'The reason, because we are here to 'talk', about us, and not him.' Veronique rebuked.

'Always...' and before Afrika could finish Mumene jumped in.

'The older and Wiser *friendcos*,' *she* said.

That closed the topic about the dashing attendant, at least for the moment.

Unaware of the recent conversation of the last few minutes, the dashing young attendant returned to serve them.

The ladies turned back to their previous conversation, their childhood and life abroad.

'I loved the games we played, and all those silly jokes and things we did together. Not sure when we shall realise our futures and dreams,' said Veronique as she took a spoon of her ice cream.

They discussed the present and the future. They were concerned about opportunities, disenfranchisement and lack of support. Sahara shared her experiences and so did the others.

'We live in different parts of the world yet we have these shared experiences?' Veronique added.

'There is a lot to worry about and when I wanted to worry about that handsome man for Afrika, you all shut me. Now you are worrying about the problems of the world.' Mumene said grudgingly.

'Mumene, this is about us, we are part of the world and with all our people scattered all over, united by colour we need to think why we are so powerless, why so disenfranchised?' Veronique added.

As the four women turned their minds to world poverty and social issues, they also thought about social and institutional structures in the society. They were concerned about opportunity and access to basic essentials by some members of the community. How their past affects and impacts on the present.

'As we consider all these things, I think we need to first learn our history to know ourselves. We need to learn about our past, we have to get it rewritten from our perspective, by us. Our youth experience challenges because they do not know who they are. We were brain washed and told that everything in the West was made of *milk and honey* and from the South, *bad*. No one taught us how the West got rich. The history of slave trade we were taught was like reading a romance novel. The slave traders were portrayed as heroes and heroines rather than as the villains they were. I mean, they did not tell us what slave trade really was and how that destroyed our communities. Unfortunately, some of our brightest minds studied only the sciences. They were never given the opportunity to learn our history. They are *blind* to our past. Their own history was never taught to them. They will never understand. The curricula designed back then, failed us. They failed to confer how our societies and our cultures were destroyed. Slave trade benefitted the traders, yet they were portrayed as our saviours. We will never know the economic cost of slavery and wars on our people. We will never know the costs of what was stolen from us, how much we lost and how much we continue to loss through debt repayments. What we know is that we survived the process, but that is not the solution. Could you imagine having a credit card debt that was half your annual income? How could you ever pay out such a credit card? You would make interest payments until the day you die, and even after that, if you're unlucky, the debt will be transferred to your next-of-kin. That is the state of some of our economies. How will they ever get out of such a debt? Let me not start on the so-called aid to developing countries. How do you knowingly help someone you know has more resources than you do? What is the logic?'

Veronique was getting agitated at that point. Sahara stepped in just in time.

'Veronique, enough said! Are you all right? Let's reflect on what you have shared and see what we can do, I mean what can the four of us do collectively. But let it not be about what went wrong in our history, let's design programs and strategies to help our people. You know, *"She who looks forward grows, she who looks only backwards stays put and dies with regrets"*. I am not going to die in sorrow; I am looking to the future. What about you Mumene, and you Afrika?'

'Veronique you spoke well, Sahara, your words are good. Now let's discuss about what is in front of us, the cheesecakes, the sticky date, the dashing waiter and ...' Mumene had not finished when Afrika stepped in.

'This cheesecake is nice Sahara.' Afrika said licking her lips.

'Johnny and I love it here. They serve good savouries and deserts.' Sahara responded.

'Yea, I can relate to that in my current state. Have a taste of my sticky date pudding'. Mumene nodded affirmatively as she stirred her plate slowly towards Sahara. 'Here, try it Sahara'.

'I must say that's one of my favourites when I come here, they do nice teas too. They're good.' Sahara said with a mouth half full of sticky date pudding.

'A nice place to close up the trip eh?' added Mumene.

They all looked at each other, leapt on their feet together as if they had it rehearsed and with one big hug and voice together they went **'Nice!'**

That night they sat and shared stories. They shed tears and they laughed together. They were all late to bed, actually very late.

After Mumene, Afrika and Veronique departed, and after a very late night, Sahara went to bed earlier than she had for the last three weeks. She missed the chats and her friends but thought it would be Wise to have an early night and good sleep. She tossed around in bed for a while before she could fall asleep.

The school she attended as a child had burned down. All the children at school on that fateful day had barely started classes when they heard loud screams from across the other end of the campus.

School children screamed, they shouted and ran. The children were scattered in every direction across the school campus. A number of them tripped over and fell; there was panic and chaos everywhere you looked.

'Activate the emergency response' came a voice from the loud speaker.

Within seconds another female's voice could be heard over the loud speaker from every corner of the school. The emergency assembly was on fire too.

'Walk, do not run, and leave your belongings behind. Leave the lunch boxes and schoolbags behind. It will be all right. We shall make available lunch for everyone. Walk to the emergency assembly grounds. Keep in mind walk, not run.' The children responded to the directives of the vice- principal on the microphone.

'Oh Lord, be of assistance to them. My family, my nieces are all there. Oh, what happened? Who lit this fire?' Sahara screamed.

The voice from the microphone suddenly started roaring again.

'The fire brigade and water tanks will be here shortly; Stay calm.' Her voice shaky as she repeated the words, 'stay calm'. 'It will be fine, soon, very soon.'

Sahara and her cousins went to this primary school and it was situated in an exclusive part of town. It would be half- an-hour before three water tanks and the fire brigade showed up. The school staff did everything in their power to calm the children as they waited. The firemen hurriedly climbed out of their trucks. Each truck had two men seated at the front.

They quickly released and pulled out the water hoses from each of their trucks. Turned them on and suddenly they turned and looked at each other.

'Dear Lord!' Shouted those with the first truck.

'This is not true!' Came a voice from the second.

'The tanks are empty? No water?' said the man from the third truck.

They sprang back into their trucks and just then a fourth truck arrived.

Two women jumped out. There was sudden silence as the women went to release their hoses. There was utter silence. All eyes were now fixed at them.

'Yeeeeehhh' could be heard everywhere across the school compound as they all cheered joyfully.

'They have water.' The children screamed.

Now realising what had happened and that the others had showed up with no water, the two women directed their hoses to the junior school block. It was adjacent to the administrative block that by now was completely in flames.

'Not in a school like this?' came a voice from the crowd.

Maybe one of the teachers or teacher aids.

Sahara saw her niece's face among the screaming children in the middle of all the chaos. The niece almost tripped. Had she fallen, others would have stampeded over her.

'Stop, walk, do not run!' Sahara screamed at her beloved niece.

Just as Sahara hopped towards her niece, she suddenly woke from her sleep. She had been dreaming.

'Phewwww!' She sighed heavily as she wiped the sweat across her forehead. 'That was close,' Sahara said as she rolled out of bed. Using her nightdress, Sahara wiped the sweat from her forehead again, feeling relieved she switched on the lights. Sahara recalled her grandfather's words about dreams. *Now, what did the dream mean?* Sahara contemplated.

'Dreams bring messages from our ancestors. What message is in this dream?' Sahara asked herself audibly.

I need to go and reconnect with my people and my land. I hope my employer will understand that I shall need time off to do that. I need to reconnect with family and roots, cousins, nieces and nephews, even those I have never met. I love them but was too far away to cuddle them and be the aunt I had hoped even if I was not like aunt Margaret.

Sahara's thoughts drifted slowly as she sank into the Louise XIV chair in her bedroom. Sahara turned to the wall on which hung some of her favourite paintings and photographs. Her attention turned to the painting of a young woman with a crown of cowries arranged in rows on her head. She had another double row of cowry strings around her wrists and another around her right ankle. Her upper body was bare, but for the cowries. She stood next to a man whose face was not visible.

His hands extended towards her. She looked at him with a smile. Her *Ankara* loincloth was simple. It was wrapped around her body from below the breast and stopped just above the knees. She had a beautiful figure; full bust and bottom, piercing brown eyes, a broad nose slightly pointed at the tip, high cheekbones with nicely shaped brows. A row of pearl white teeth perfected her features. A subtle smile adorned her face as she looked toward the man extending his hand towards her. Her right hand slightly extended towards his left as they looked to each other. Her right arm partly covered her breast and nipples. There was a tear in her left eye.

Sahara focused on the portrait. She loved to look at the fresh face of the young woman in this painting. It was as if her sorrows melted or just vanished whenever she set eyes on it. Sahara looked at the portrait every day and she admired it even more every time she did.

'Oh relocation, migration. Its joys and challenges.' Sahara spoke to herself as she started her daily routine.

It was now 6:00 am. The old silver alarm clock chimed. 'Get up, wake up, it's time to rise.'

Feeling annoyed, still visibly shaken by her dream, Sahara turned off the alarm.

'Clocks, alarms, who made them?' She rolled her eyes as she repeated the words to herself.

Tears rolled down Sahara cheeks. Her nose ran.

She grabbed a tissue from the box next to her, blew hard and then wiped her nose. She blew hard again into the tissue *to get rid of the entire snot in there. While snot can look grubby, it is actually good for you; it traps the dust and other small foreign participles from entering your body. Even something that we may dislike has such an important role. What about someone who may look, sound and act different to you? They all have a place and deserve one.* Sahara tried to push these thoughts to the back of her mind. They kept resurfacing in different ways. *I shall call Afrika or Veronique and Mumene later to discuss this. I am exhausted with the negative energy at work. Now this dream affirms my greatest fears. It had fire. Will I be fired?*

At the same time, she wondered about her family.

'Was it worth it leaving them?'

'Is the money worth missing all the family birthdays, weddings, and funerals?'

The call proved to be worthwhile as these people knew her well. What it did though was to evoke those memories Sahara wanted to suppress at such moments.

Veronique had decided to move to live Australia but lived in the Northern Territory.

Veronique's mother, Ma Terrie had worked for the influential family of the 'Honourable.' *As for Afrika, Veronique's sister by birth, that girl, must have been born on a bright sunny day. The sun must have been rising. She's beautiful, ebony smooth. Never touched any of that hydroquinone bleaching nonsense on her body. That's my girl. She thought. But who was Afrika's Father? No one ever spoke about it. Yes, Ma Terrie was their mother, we know the rumour about Veronique's father, what about Afrika?* Sahara pushed the thoughts away from her mind.

Prior to moving to Australia, Veronique had been in Europe studying. She received a scholarship from a wealthy anonymous donor when she graduated. She had learnt Hungarian, completed a master's degree in accounting and law before relocating to Australia as a professional.

These four lady friends had a common vision and purpose – the drive to succeed.

How they had all changed over the last two decades, both physically and mentally. They had separated after completing their first year of undergraduate studies. They went abroad for further studies. Certain aspects of their lives had not changed. They still loved to engage with each other, have fun and go out together. That last trip to the mall was just so beautiful, spending quality time with my allies. We could all cry on each other shoulders without fear or shame. It had been a good time. Everyone should have someone like that in his or her life. I feel better whenever I speak to these three friends or see them. I have however struggled to connect with others at the same level since we migrated.

Despite the physical distance, Sahara, Mumene and Veronique had a shared childhood. The bond between them remains. They had someone they all admired too, a woman they loved and cared about, Aunty Margaret.

CHAPTER 4

Aunty Margaret and Akornde

Society, they now agreed had failed her. Rigid norms and structures had let her down, but Margaret refused to let herself and her children down. She was a woman with purpose and a woman of action. She worked hard, but with little returns. She was teased and she almost caved in until the day the big bully stood in her way. *I must stop him,* she told herself. That was what caught the imagination of other young women. Margaret, the introverted illiterate girl, a heroine?

Veronique and Sahara were always in some sort of trouble. Mumene and Afrika slightly gentler were still mischievous and often did some really obtuse things. Sahara invariably led the pack. She got into mishaps that were always so real; like the day the new boy arrived midterm at their high school. All eyes were on him. He was tall, and had beautiful eyes, a kind smile, big, tall with dark Afro hair. He was masculine. The girls lined up for his attention. Sahara was barely sixteen at the time.

The second week after his arrival Sahara ran to catch up with Veronique after school. They walked together to the designated spot where their driver would pick them up and take them home.

'Veronique, Veronique, you'll never guess. I have news… for you' Sahara called out.

Veronique recognised the voice and turned around immediately.

'Hello. What's it about?'

'Guess…'

'You aced your math's test.'

'Well, that's expected. Something more exciting.'

'Your mum bought you something, a new pair of shoes, watch?'

'Okay, clue, 'dude in school.' I mean the handsome one.'

'He's smart. Aced his maths test too?'

'More.'

'Interested in that Susan? She gets all the attention?

'Nope.'

'Okay, please tell me'

'Last guess.'

'They held hands today?'

'He kept looking at me in class. That is why you did not see me at lunch. 'Then, what happened?' by now Veronique was becoming inpatient.

'Well, we sat back and discussed the maths tests results. He did well too, not like me though.'

'Hmmm?'

'Then he leaned forward and ...'

Before Sahara could finish her sentence, Veronique jumped in.

'Oh, it did not happen, he gave you peck Sahara?'

'Not quite a peck, the K Word Yep.'

'Kiss?'

The news of the kiss went around the school like wild fire. Susan had seen them and felt Sahara had cheated her. It was *big news*.

'Sahara you did not.'

'Well didn't we all want it? And Susan?'

'That is disgusting; the likelihood that you, Sahara could fall sick is high.

That was what Aunty Margaret had told the kids if they went close to boys, let alone *'touch'* them.

The role of aunties was 'sacred' and people like the gentle, sage but firm Aunty Margaret was important within a family and community. Despite her youthful age of thirty-five, her role within the community was well acknowledged. A mother to four children, Aunty Margaret was alert and the local girls and nieces trusted her with their secrets. They believed in her and she always protected and guided them when either was warranted. The teenagers considered her words gold, whether they made sense or not. Margaret a shrewd listener and counsellor kept secrets meticulously.

Aunty Margaret had never married; was considered a free woman. The freemen on other hand were never spoken of. Yes, they were men and she, well 'just' a woman. No one really knew the father of her children, yet she had four children. There were always the rumours and suspicion. She was free, beautiful, intelligent, a hard worker and STURDY. One would think a woman like her should have a stream of suitors. After the first unplanned pregnancy while unwedded that was it. It did not bother her impregnator. He never showed up again and was never spoken of again. Margaret on the contrary having 'disgraced' herself and her family was gossiped about endlessly. She had brought her and her family disfavour and dishonour; that was the view of the older generation. The younger generation perceived Margaret differently.

The younger girls recognized Margaret as their heroine, a no 'nonsense' woman who did what she wanted when she wanted. She worked hard to send her children to private schools. She was spiritual too, an unlikely trait for a free woman.

Aunty Margaret had counselled Sahara, Veronique, Mumene and Afrika to keep away from all the boys.

Sahara recalled when Aunty Margaret sat her down. She remembers unmistakably that she sat on a low stool made from bamboo, while the girls sat on a mat in a semicircle in front of her. Aunty Margaret sipped tea as she addressed them. They all were fixed on her. Sahara, Veronique and her friends listened without question. After all, it was Aunty Margaret speaking. Their parents did not know their children had these meetings with Margaret. They would never have approved of Margaret being a mentor to their daughters. The disparity could not be more dissimilar: different backgrounds, different social and economic status. It was like chalk and cheese yet they lived closely. Afrika and Veronique were somehow benefitting from their mother's employer. Ma Terrie their mother was not married, but she worked for Madam and Honourable.

As they sat quietly, Margaret commenced, 'Children you know, school is good. Go and *open your eyes*. This world is full of devils. Be careful; be careful especially with the boys. They fool you and that's it.'

Sahara asked, 'how? Why?'

'They are 'bad' for girls like you Sahara and you, and you and you.' Margaret using her index finger, pointed to each of the girls as she spoke.

Veronique also asked, 'how?'

Margaret, eyes narrowed and with a deep frown, stiff upper lip, deep voice with a firm tone said, 'look at me, the boys *spoilt* me.'

Back then, Afrika and Veronique did not understand what she meant.

Mumene with questioning eyes said, 'how Aunty?'

All four girls searched in their minds *how could boys have spoilt a woman like her?* They were both intrigued and perplexed by such a statement. *A tough beauty like Aunty Margaret, how could that be?*

Margaret, who had taught Akornde a lesson no one imagined? Akornde, the bully dared call her 'free' and wanted a relationship with her. By then she was a mother to one son. Her snotty behaviour towards Akornde made him feel mediocre. A firewood chopper and tapper with big strong hands, Akornde looked every bit the wrestler. His imposing stature frightened many. He had pounced on many a woman, and men at times. He always got what he wanted. He was feared. Akornde was a mean bully. Reporting him to the elders was received with deaf ears. They had adjudicated too many Akornde matters and they feared for their families, especially their daughters if the case did go against Akornde. The *Ndiys (elders)* often elected to abstain rather than intervene in matters that concerned Akornde. This Goliath of a man was a self-made king; he lived by his own rules.

Margaret, a seemingly innocent girl selling groundnuts was not your ordinary girl. She had ignored Akornde's advances for a long time. She had been one of the first girls to caution him to stop.

Today, there was a football match between two student teams. July, boast the youth week and all the youth aged between thirteen and twenty-five except for Munga, who at 37 considered himself one of the youth came together to interact, and to learn and celebrate culture. He had never been a student; youth or cultural week was about students returning home during the summer holidays to help with the harvest and learn the culture. It was not so much culture that they learnt, as it was an opportunity to get off the claws of parents and hang out late with others of similar age, with likeminded ideas.

Girls like Margaret who had not had the opportunity to finish secondary school used this time to make as much money as they could by selling groundnuts, sweets, beignet, gateaux and other local delicacies. The students came home for cultural week cashed up; well they may have saved their twenty dollars equivalent sometimes more if their parents added some extra. For students that was a lot of money.

Margaret, a savvy entrepreneur, maximised her profits during this week. She would stock up weeks prior and increased the price of whatever she sold. She was good at what she did. If she had the opportunity to attend and complete school, she would have fulfilled her dream of being a sports teacher. She could run faster than all the boys in class when she was in primary school, played football with boys and was just as good as them. Looking at her, she had the deceptive appearance of a gentle kind-hearted kitten.

On that fateful day in the field, she took Akornde unaware when he approached her for the third time. It was a demand from Akornde to Margaret.

'I want marriage, Margaret.' He loved her, longed for her and desired her, he would say. Margaret truly detested him with a passion. Upon hearing this Margaret's head spun:

'Who weds an idiot? A control freak! At what level in life was I now for such a fool to even contemplate a lifelong relationship with me?' Margaret grunted to herself. *I must do something about it sooner rather than later.*

Margaret took Akornde by surprise. The kicking and hard knocks could not get rid of her firm grip. They struggled and rolled around. Within minutes there was a crowd and a match referee. The referee shouted, 'leave them alone.' The referee was the town jester. 'Let a woman show this man, teach him his first lesson. No one had dared before,' he shouted. By now Margaret had Akornde rolling in the mud. It was a mud bath. As the crowd grew, claps accompanied jeers, aimed at Akornde, and grew louder and more deafening by the minute.

Not one person dared to interfere, as it appeared the woman had the upper hand.

How could they go near Akornde? How could they even think of going near him?

The jeering and cheering became louder and louder. Not in decades had people of Muka seen wrestling competitions. The missionaries had outlawed wrestling some five decades earlier. Only the older generation had memories of the village-wrestling heroes.

Today without any warning they were being entertained with a wrestling match, a special match and a rarity; a unique incidence. Not two men as was the norm but a woman with a man. Not any man; Akornde, the village tyrant. Well, after this match their genders could easily be reversed.

The *village vine* was in a meltdown too. Gossip spread like wildfire through the village vine. Today's social media was not required to get the news out.

Akornde had intimidated many local children. He seemed to get pleasure out of it. Well, today Margaret was giving him that same pleasure; only it was in a mud puddle. She couldn't care less. For those standing by, Margaret was simply doing a job. Many onlookers had hoped for and dreamed for this day to come. Finally, it was happening right in front of them. That day finally came. It was like children waiting for Santa Claus on Christmas Eve. The difference was that Santa's December arrival, though exciting, was expected. Today on the contrary was a complete surprise in every aspect of the word, that's what made it more exciting. This had never happened before. A woman on top of Akornde was inconceivable! Akornde struggled to get rid of her. Flick him off like a fly. Blow the butterfly away. Margaret's hands were stuck on him like glue. Margaret successfully pulled down his torn slacks and because they were so old and worn, they gave way effortlessly. As she pulled them down, she screamed at the same time, Akornde screamed and pulled in the opposite direction. '*Abihza*, my cargo, my testes, I'm dead' Akornde cried.

The place went into meltdown when he uttered the word Abihza, jeering and clapping. God seemed to have heard Margaret's prayers and that of the crowd. Even a thief prays when they go to rob someone. Why shouldn't Margaret do the same on this unique day? Within seconds Akornde's pants were gone.

He was in his 'birthday suit' from waist down. Except for the upper half of his body, he was the way he came into the world. Instead of meconium all over him, he was covered in mud.

Akornde had no underpants.

He never wore them because he liked to be 'free'. He was a 'free' man. Underpants cost money too.

Today he was completely 'free'; Margaret had his 'cargo' on show.

It was a public show.

The balls were in the air and he was in complete 'commando' form. Margaret stood up, and with her right hand held Akornde pants, her share of the remnants in the air.

Using only two fingers in the left hand, she beckoned Akornde to turn and to move closer.

As he rolled and laid face down for some privacy, his buttocks were completely exposed. As he used both hands to cover up his 'cargo', Margaret placed her left foot on his right buttock.

He wriggled but both hands were 'on duty'. He was salvaging what he could and protecting whatever dignity he had left.

Using both hands he held unto his penis and testes tight.

They could not fit in both hands.

By this time the crowd was not only large but had gone wild.

Their thundering voices could be heard kilometres away.

This was all happening in the middle of the football field. It was the middle of the day, bright daylight. Everyone could see what was happening.

For those who still had their eardrums intact, the noise was still deafening.

The young and old, men and women alike, screamed at the top of their voices.

'Not in my life time, I did not imagine such a thing to Akornde.'

'A woman with breast on her chest, 'shakes' up a man like a snake?'

'Not any man either,' added another bystander. 'Akornde,' he said as he hit his own chest with the open palm of his left hand, while he moved his head from side-to-side.

'The strong man is on the ground,' added another.

It was instant celebration.

It was sweet victory especially as it was unexpected.

Not even Margaret could have imagined this scene. As if that was not enough, Margaret gathered the courage to ask him to stand up right.

He obeyed without question.

He must have imagined what may befall him if he did not obey this woman.

The crowd was yet to watch the real movie; that had been the trailer and the biggest fight was yet to come. This fight was not about blows. It was a mental fight, a feline fight that people could only have dreamt of. How could anyone imagine

Akornde in a fight with a woman? They did what he told them always without question. The one woman who had defied him, reversed the roles. He was obeying without question.

His words used to be command.

At this moment, her words were not only command, but law.

Men, women, boys and girls, young and old feared this man. He may have been fierce and fearless; now he had met his match in his heroine, Margaret.

Margaret with a stern grin in her face, her heart pounding like women pounding *achu*, (a traditional dish made from pounded varieties of *cocoyams* and green bananas) stood akimbo. One hand on the hip, pants in the other, she waited for Akornde to look at her in the eyes.

You could hear her heart pounding from two metres away, and her breathing was like that of an athlete after an 800 meters' sprint. Margaret fumed with anger, but she beamed with pride inside. She felt confident and the crowd's energy was completely behind her. Margaret felt like David. With Goliath now up, looking like a pig after a mud bath, Margaret waited and was ready to pounce if he did not oblige her.

Akornde the Goliath, now on his feet, head bowed, large balls in both palms, penis dangling, looked like a rat that had just been rescued from the teeth of a hungry cat. He was motionless and emotionless.

Only that this cat was still hungry, and leapt towards Goliath, who was more focused on protecting his package.

The crowd cheered; every cheer, seemed to give this lady another surge of energy.

She pulled his hands apart to expose the whole package.

Finally, Goliath, Akornde the strong man had been humbled.

Not even he could believe his fate.

He thought it must have been a nightmare, but it had really happened.

Margaret, the quiet, gentle, athletic girl, had stamped her name in the book of heroines. She was a *Shero*.

From that day forth, if Akornde dared put a foot wrong, he was teased or called Margaret.

Unfortunately, teenagers are not too kind with such people. Whenever they saw him, the name 'Margaret' would be promptly used in a sentence regardless of the topic. They would say the word MARGARET to Akornde's hearing.

That was over two decades ago, when Margaret had humbled the *bully*. Sahara and Veronique though very young at the time, recall how people had gathered in their homestead to compliment Margaret. No one who had been alive then could forget that day. It was still fresh in their memories as if it only happened yesterday. It changed Akornde forever. How could it not?

The young Margaret became 'Aunty' Margaret for many young women. She had joined the ranks of the elders. Youth were judged on capabilities rather than on their age. Margaret deserved respect and to be within the ranks of elders.

Margaret had provided justice to many who knew they would never get any, nor matter what they did. Justice, they said came in many forms, and for many she had given the Goliath a life sentence. Because of her, they would not have to live in fear;

forever they will be grateful. As for Akornde he was humbled forever.

Margaret, a beautiful local maiden, was now a Shero. A school dropout, after her parent's death was now a celebrated person. Her grandmother had been unable to afford the fees at the local Christian school.

The uncles advised her grandmother that Margaret was almost ripe for marriage anyway. Her aunt affirmed this position. No one wanted her; she would be a burden for them and their families should they take her in.

Margaret fell pregnant shortly after, while unwedded. She was only sixteen then, a child having a child. She was shunned.

She had to make adult decisions for her and her baby. She became fearless but focused; she refused to allow other girls to follow her path, by force or by choice. She loved them and protected them. Her word was gospel as far as these 'nieces' and young maidens were concerned. So, when she counselled Veronique, Sahara, Mumene and Afrika, they believed her. Margaret had walked the road before them.

CHAPTER 5

The Kiss and the Wise fool

Sahara also looked up to Veronique, her counsellor who was also a year older than her, therefore Wiser. Veronique had gone into panic mode upon hearing the news of the kiss.

To cleanse Sahara of the kiss curse, the trio - Sahara, Afrika and Mumene secretly visited a Wise man to discuss the dilemma and what evil may befall Sahara because of the kiss. The *Wise man* used his shells to consult the gods of the land.

As the girls walked in, the Wise man sitting in a corner inside the poorly lit room, hummed quietly alone.

He spoke in 'tongues'. The girls heard murmurs but understood nothing that he said.

Through the Wise man, the gods communicated a message to Sahara. She was 'never to touch another male until marriage.' If she did, 'she would never bear children,' she was told. Motherhood is something that young women are socialised to accept from an early age. Society, especially in interdependent communities, revolves around children and family. For Sahara to be faced with such a predicament was a perceived calamity.

'A girl has to have a family.' Sahara could hear her mother's voice inside her head.

Children, who cares? she tried dismissing the voice and her thoughts.

'Did you say 'who cares'?' Sahara mother's voice was even stronger after this.

Sahara tried hard to ignore the voice; the more she tried, the louder and worse it became.

The witches or Wise women were said to be responsible for infertility.

Wise women, unlike Wise men were treated differently. This had prompted their decision not to go to the, Wise woman, up the hill.

She lived there with seven children; some adopted, others fostered, because they were unwanted at birth or had lost their mothers. Maternal deaths remain a serious problem for this community. *How could she be a Wise woman?* Sahara wondered.

The Wise man finally lifted his head and listened to the girls.

Sahara spoke first.

'My mother will kill me, I kissed a boy,' Sahara started.

'No, a boy kissed you,' Afrika jumped in.

'That's correct,' nodded Mumene.

The Wise man listened while the girls debated what the right words were among themselves. Mumene, sitting with her left elbow on her knee using her palm to cover her mouth and nose, finally let out her thoughts. 'What a smell?'

'Ssssshhhhh…' Sahara responded, and with her index finger over her lips, eyes firmly fixed at her friend, Sahara stared sternly at her.

'That is a big problem. How could you do this to your family? Did your mother not tell you or teach you how to behave around boys?' The Wise man rebuked Sahara harshly then continued. 'The gods are angry.' He repeated this twice as he threw his shells in the air and they landed all over the floor. He repeated this a few more times, and each time the shells would form a different pattern.

'You all need to be protected, but you,' pointing at Sahara, 'have to be cleansed. I shall need three large kola nuts in their pots, a black hen and a white cock. I can also accept money; fifty thousand CFA will do. Do you know *dorrah* (dollar)? One hundred dorrah will be fine.'

Upon hearing this, the girls turned to face each other.

They stared at each other for a minute, no words uttered.

Sahara had her hands over her cheeks as if to support her heavy head. Her head was in fact very heavy, it was full of problems that were beyond her and she had no idea how to resolve them.

'Did you hear that, Afrika?'

'I did, Sahara. What about you, Mumene?'

'Yes.' Eyebrows lifted and eyes open.

'Okay' Sahara nodded to the Wise man as she walked to the door.

The others followed, visibly shaken by the request.

'What are you going to do Sahara?' Mumene asked

'Errrrr, don't know,' Sahara replied as she scratched her head.

The girls had to come up with a plan, and soon. The *Wise man* had spoken and 'the gods were angry with Sahara.' They raised various ideas, but none seemed to cut through. They all had to agree on a common solution. After all, they were in this together! At home the girls continued to contemplate on ideas.

'Let's start a business and sell homemade sweets at school,' Afrika proposed.

'Groundnut sweets will be better?' Sahara added. 'At least we can make them ourselves. Mum stocks groundnuts and sugar at home. We can just take some, she will never notice. She has no idea what is in the food store. Ma Terrie is the only one that enters the store room and we can work with her on this.' Afrika proposed.

'Don't even think it! Even Madam fears Ma Terrie though she is the maid. Believe me, I have seen it.' Mumene responded with a smile.

When Veronique later heard about the day's events, she too was concerned. These four worried about each other, and what concerned one person, affected all of them.

'Sahara, how long will that take us to raise the money?' Veronique asked.

'A few months, maybe a school term?'

'What are we going to say at home? They won't let you; you know that! You know your mother and father! Convincing your mother about anything is like trying to climb Mount Everest.'

'Okay, I get it. So, what do you want me to do? I mean us?'

Veronique suggested they sell fresh fruits in front of her father's mansion to make the extra cash. To her, it was achieving something for herself and making some pocket money without receiving the usual handout from mum and dad. She thought her parents would be proud of her for attempting to do something for herself. She thought of Mamie Murphy who sold fruits only a stone's throw away from her father's mansion.

Mamie Murphy lived in a wooden two-bedroom *karaboat* that leaned against the two-metre fence of Honourable's mansion. The fence surrounded the two hectares of land his father had purchased from

Mamie Murphy's father-in-law many years ago. The house was almost *see through*, from wear-and-tear, and the woman used old newspapers and cement packaging to plug the holes. The roof leaked when it rained. The house was in a 'sorry' state. As a widow, she sold fruits to sustain her family. This was her only source of income; she was determined to make a better life for her children. Her children assisted with the family business whenever possible. Every room in their home had a small hanging fluorescent bulb. At least it provided her children with some reasonable lighting to study at home and complete their homework. Close by, were Honourable and his friends, whose lives and that of their children was the exact opposite to that of Mamie Murphy and her children.

'Birds of the same feather flock together' they say. None of their children 'worked'. They had the house helps, the drivers to take them to and from school, the gardeners. Their house chores, if any at all were limited to their tidying their bedrooms, which were never tidy unless the maid did it. The way the people next door lived, was only imaginable to Mamie Murphy and her family. Though so close, their lives were miles apart. Mamie Murphy promised her children that they would never lead her life of poverty while she still had her two hands to work, could walk and could see. Such wealth disparities are sometimes unimaginable, yet the affluent are comfortable within these structures. However, the children of the poor tended to benefit without realising from the constant presence of their parents.

The girls had to think fast and act soon.

'This kiss curse is really serious and we need to go back to the Wise man. Let's sell some belongings?' Veronique suggested as a last resort.

'Mum (*Madam*) and dad (*Honourable*) will not notice. They are too busy. Dad has no idea what I have anyway!' Said Sahara.'

Veronique did not support the idea, saying, 'Ma Terrie, will notice and will tell your mother.'

Mother was commonly referred to as 'Madam' in her local community because of her husband's and family's affluential status.

Ma Terrie, short for Tereszja, was the housemaid and she mothered madam's children. She almost single handedly raised those children. Not once did their dad drop off or pick them up from school; it was not considered manly, particularly for such an important man. Honourable was an *important* person; to pick up his own children from school was not the role for such a high-status person. That was the driver's job.

Mumene, recalls going for days without any sight of her Honourable, dad, though they lived together under the same roof. They children entered his living areas only when invited; they got into trouble if otherwise, and even Madam got into trouble when without special reason went to her husband's bedroom. He went to her when he was 'free' and invited her, when the main family's shared area was open to his guests. Not his private quarters. Mumene wondered, as she got older how her parents could live the way they did. Why would her mother accept such an arrangement? Would her father have accepted it if their roles were reversed? Mumene, would never know the answer. Such realities drew her attention to the pernicious gender imbalances and structures that were deeply ingrained in her community.

Madam was blamed for the children's unruliness. A former high school teacher, Madam stopped working when Honourable married her. He did not want his wife to work. Theirs had been an accidental encounter. She was constantly reminded of the privileges she enjoyed because of Honourable. She detested this, but never complained. Her less privileged siblings pitied Madam because they thought she experienced emotional abuse daily. She never left home without Honourable's permission including the return time. A driver was always on hand to pick up and drop her. They were more than drivers, perhaps bodyguards, or worse: spies for Honourable. Money, she had, freedom was the question. Her husband often reminded Madam that it was for her own safety and protection; after all, she was his wife and he was responsible for her.

Honourable was revered but dreaded within his household and that sometimes extended to the community. When he called you in as a child, it sent shivers down your spine. For the young girls who worked there, they had reasons to shiver, especially from a 'skirt lifter' like him. Honourable was a lecher.

His notoriety was known but no one spoke of it. He was important and untouchable.

Ma Terrie, Madam's favourite and longest serving maid, was one he couldn't stand. She was dutiful but fearless; humble but stood her ground. She had been responsible for exposing two of the secret children fathered by Honourable with his mistresses.

Honourable feared one person only within the household, Ma Terrie. For some reason, Honourable could be excessively kind to Ma Terrie and her children. Her younger children mingled with his, though not at Madam's approval. But Madam was too afraid to disapprove of the children's friendship openly, not when Honourable was so fond of one of them.

Did Ma Terrie hold other secrets? Madam often wondered.

As Ma Terrie helped Madam around the house, the girls still busy hatching a plan for how to raise the much-needed funds without they raising any alarm bells. It was their secret. They also at this point thought of Aunty Margaret but were too scared to share the kiss incident with her. She had always been firm about not kissing any boy, now Sahara had done just that.

What do I do? Thought Sahara

'Sahara what do you think? You know my green leather jacket, the one I got for my fourteenth birthday? Maybe we sell it or better still set up a small stall outside the house? Mamie Murphy does it. I will let mother know; they should see it as a sign of my entrepreneurial skills development.'

Mumene's request was met with a firm 'no, no further questions asked,' her father had grunted. Yet only a few metres away from his mansion, was Mamie Murphy with a fruit stall.

Mamie Murphy sold pawpaw, oranges and other fruits. Mumene's father bought apples, oranges, mangoes, watermelon and other fruits from Mamie Murphy often when he returned from work.

'Mamie Murphy, bring me two pineapples, one water melon and two papaws.' Honourable requested.

'Yes, sir, you do not want some oranges today?'

'Mamie Murphy, you take all my money here all the time'

'Thank you, sir, you want the sweet mangoes too? I got some passion fruit today.'

Honourable's driver paid for the fruits and they drove off.

'These fruits are getting expensive. This woman must be making a *killing* from me. She knows I like fruits'.

'What a good idea! We will pay the Wise man and get some left over. You can have my orange leather baseball hat to include in this project if that helps.'

'But who is going to pay for it? It's expensive, my father had told me. Everyone had seen me in this. Who would want to be thought of as borrowing or begging, or worse, wearing hand me downs?'

Not a tag these *'rich affluenzas'* and their circle of friends wished for.

The girls were happy when a cousin, Erika, came to spend part of her summer holidays with her Godmother, Madam. Only a few days after her arrival, Sahara and Veronique approached her with a seemingly nice sale.

'Erika, you know as you said you wanted some stuff before leaving? One of our friends is selling some leather goods. They are really nice, a bit expensive but we can talk to her.' Sahara opened the conversation.

'I am not sure. Do I have enough money to buy anything like that leather jacket? Don't they cost like many thousands CFA?'

'Erika, she is our *friend* and it will be something different for you to take with you.' Veronique added.

'Do I need a leather jacket in that hot climate? When will I even get to use it?'

Veronique and Sahara stared at each other. A period of silence ensued.

'Okay then, do not worry about it; we shall get some else to buy it. Your loss!' Snapped Veronique as she stood up and walked out, leaving the other two alone.

'Erika, have a think about it; if you buy it, you can sell it at full price over there. You will make a profit. So, you will have your money back, plus extra.'

'I'll think about it Sahara.'

'I agree, think about it.'

Both girls stood up and left the room.

Erika thought to herself, *no one would know the items were not new after I return home.* Home was another 200km away.

Erika loved her cousins. Though she did not need the items, and may never wear them, she purchased them to make them happy.

I may never wear the leather jacket, but may use the baseball hat, Erika convinced herself. What she did not know was why they so badly wanted to sell the jacket.

The next day Sahara and Veronique returned to the Wise man with the money rather than the black hen and a white cock.

They forgot about the kolanuts or they simply ignored it. The Wise man could hardly belief the girls returned with the money within such a short period. He normally took months to make such amounts.

He welcomed them, took the money, and starred at the girls.

'What do your parents do?'

'My father is Honourable and my mother is Madam, replied Sahara.

'I know who they are.'

'Yes, everyone around here knows them, but they did not give us this money. They shouldn't know we came here. They don't even know we know you exist anyway.

'Everyone knows me. Madam was here before getting married to Honourable'

At that moment the girls' hearts sank into their stomachs. How could Madam enter such a place? *Did the Wise man have something to do with Madam and Honourable's relationship?* Sahara pondered.

'Where are the other items?'

'I can add 10,000 CFA, if that helps'.

'Yes,' he grunted in response.

'Here, take.' Veronique handed him the money.

'Sit down on that stool next to the white feathers,' He directed Sahara. He did not ask for the kolanuts. Did he forget what he needed himself?

The girls obeyed without question.

The Wise man got a calabash. He poured out about ten millilitres of its contents as he murmured to himself.

'Now take this; when you turn the corner on your left, throw it as far as you can. Walk straight home and do not speak to anyone. Never return again,' He said as he handed Sahara ten shells.

Today as grownups, they laughed loudly at themselves. How ignorant were they? How the world has changed! How could they have been fooled so easily by an aunt but even more oblivious by that Wise fool?'

'Really, he was a 'scammer'. How many other people did he cheat?'

'Oh dear; if he only knew the lengths we went to, so we could raise the funds. Poor Erika! That scammer, Wise fool perhaps, made us take money from the innocent girl and hand over to him. He must have collected those shells, he made me throw, immediately after we turned the first corner.'

'Veronique, if you one day pull that out to your unborn children, I bet you they will ask Wise man Google. Maybe the

App is not even here, yet.' Mumene added.

'They would laugh at us if you dared pull out such a stunt about boyfriends from Aunty Margaret's rule book.'

'How technology took over us, Veronique?'

'Ingenious one; Ignoramus we were back then!' Cried Afrika.

'What if we had gone to a Wise woman instead, Veronique?'

'Oh dear, Afrika, I feel silly even now when I think of it,' cried Veronique.

Thoughts of the Wise woman came rushing through their minds. They wondered what happened to her and all those children. She had simply disappeared in thin air. Rumours had it that she 'ate all the children' then disappeared into the forest. Rumours, rumours, they destroy society.

Childhood memories returned back after the visits by Veronique, Mumene and Afrika. She was happy but drained by the endless activities. *Why it is called 'holidays' when one did not actually rest?* Sahara wondered.

'I loved every minute of it,' she reminded herself while dismissing her inner voice.

Part two

CHAPTER 6

The struggles

Sahara now living abroad, grieved over recent events in her home country.

The Pianes fighting their neighbours and the Nganes worries me. How could people from these two tribes, who speak and understand each other, who share the same cultures and a god, fight each other? This was happening back in their home countries and was affecting those living abroad. Can we continue to pretend what happens there does not affect us out here? Can I trust someone from the Ngane tribe? Africa is rising, yet not much is being spoken about that too. Why?'

All these questions went through Sahara's mind. She was quite distressed about all the 'politics', worried about media representations of people of colour. Not always positive, yet their success stories were actually not dissimilar to those of others. She had to change that. It affected many aspects of her life and the lives of many people she knew. Sahara worried about her children, and her future grandchildren if such narratives do not change. *We must tell African stories, the way we want, from an Afrocentric perspective. We have to narrate these our way and as they happen. That's the only way our future can be safely guaranteed. Thank God we have so much talent within us. If only the world accepted that, because I cannot say, they don't know the reality. Actually, there are a few ignoramuses out there who outright refuse to accept us, and our place in history. We cannot accept that, and we cannot let that be. We must think about the queens of the African empires, the kings and the soldiers who stood up, those who successfully dismantled colonisation, but in reality, only physical, because economic and psychological colonisation continues.* Sahara began to sob after these thoughts.

What's more important; my capabilities or the 'shade' of my skin? Does it matter?

This African Gang phenomenon! Seriously are these hard-working citizens criminals? What about all the professionals I know and hang out with? Teachers, doctors, nurses, chemists, electricians and entrepreneurs, and the list go on. What about them? Why are they not in the media? They are actually the majority. And my friend who is an actuary and the other who is specialising in brain surgery? I bet none of those hyping this

#AfricanGang thing know of them or do they simply ignore the truth?

Sahara thought of her parent's words to her. 'Sahara you are intelligent, have better opportunities, make the most of it my child.' They would caution her.

Her grandfather; 'if you are gifted, help others. Use your gift to do that.' Those words never left Sahara.

In recent times she is disillusioned by the rhetoric on skin colour and crime. But as Sahara learnt about her history, she realised how sheltered she had been. These things are not new; they are historical, and her people have felt suppressed for generations. It's like living in bondage without the chains.

What are the underlying causes of crime?

Sahara like many others did not like to consider herself a failure. She loved home, but the current state of events caused her great anxiety. There was a civil uprising, as the locals demanded more for their ancestral land that had been handed over to a multinational company. They wanted their land back or are properly compensated for it. *But who was more corrupt, those that take bribes openly or those that use economic structures, institutional and policies to impoverish the majority?*

Sahara's father was a victim of such brutality. He had died mysteriously in custody. He was vocal and had stood up for his people. He was prepared to die for the cause of his people. 'Our land is our life. It is money, it's where we come from,' and *'the earth is your god,'* he would say at meetings. 'Land means water, food, our animals and it is our home. Without land we have nothing. We shall remain in poverty and will never know what freedom is.'

Sahara had returned home after her studies but when war broke out in her homeland, she found herself in an anarchic place. An accountant from an affluential family, life was now completely different to what she knew. She made the brave decision to leave against her family's wishes. They stayed behind. Now her father was gone.

The news came as a shock to Sahara, though she was not surprised. She knew her father was a brave man and she understood the fate that awaited those who spoke up. Even at her workplace in a Western country, there were real risks for doing such, what about in her home? Those risks were real, and for her father the cost was his life.

Sahara's father had been arrested while she was away; he died mysteriously three weeks later in custody. He was buried within hours after his demise. No post mortem. *Who was to blame for the lack of, accountable structures and institutions?* What did my people do to God? Yet they pray more that everyone I know! They must strategize and redirect their prayers to the unfeigned god, their tribal gods, maybe. *The current god that was brought to them does not seem to answer the prayers of the majority. Does this new god speak their language?*

I resent the current state of scrutiny and marginalisation of colour.

Ahbotta's voice startled Sahara who was deep in thought.

'There is breakfast on the table Sahara.'

'Thank you Ahbotta, I was in a faraway land when you called. I was thinking of my people. Our people.'

Ahbotta, decided not to respond. Instead she walked out slowly. She understood Sahara and knew she had to leave her alone during such moments.

A mother to four children, two sets of twins, identical girls and identical boys, Sahara, a double *manyi* (mother of twins), wanted to be a model mother and parent for her children. She got up early and worked hard daily but felt unfulfilled. How do I use the skills I have, apply them to a job I want, without being seen to be a nuisance or an ambitious witch? *Why do ambitious women get called names?* 'I hate what I do at the moment. It has to change and it's only me who can change that;' Sahara reminded herself in a loud voice.

She often referred to her current work as mindless for an *A* grade graduate like herself, someone with a double Master's degree in law and accounting. She could have done any degree she wanted because she scored well in her Advance levels exams: five *A* grades. How could she justify packing toilet seats in a factory with those qualifications, and being supervised by someone like the current supervisor? *If only my country was stable! Here I am and cannot return and cannot live the life I want! I hate those slayers called leaders! Here I am working under someone with concrete thoughts and attitudes and nothing beyond.*

Sahara's supervisor had barely made it while in school; he was an average student but possessed the networks. Now an executive, he seemed to be out of his depth, being over-promoted. He had climbed the corporate ladder in his firm too speedily. His father had worked in the same industry, so had his uncle and grandfather. His family name was well known in the firm. By forty he was already a senior manager, and by forty-three an executive director. He was aiming for the CEO position by the time he reached fifty. Only one more level before he got the top job; he had the code to the ceiling. There was no stopping him, though he was not the most capable or qualified for the role.

Why? I wished I was coded in similar fashion. I know I can only wish and dream; maybe someday, Sahara deliberated.

Hers, she knew was neither the glass nor the bamboo ceiling. Sahara created her own equation:

Gender + accent + colour = Unemployment + under employment + no promotion. Period.

Following the uprising, after Sahara's return from abroad and within seven short months of commencing practice in a reputable firm, Sahara found herself in a refugee camp. She hoped it would be for a few weeks. Weeks became months and months became years. Sahara would loss three productive years in Samaku refugee camp. While in Samaku, Sahara would think of her previous life, her family status, and lament, 'I now live like Mamie Murphy.' Samaku was in the middle of nowhere. Its residents had nothing but hope, more hope, and resilience. With none of her family there, Sahara relied on the goodwill of friends and neighbours. Sahara's beloved home country was torn apart by what was now a civil war. Her family was now completely separated.

Sahara's country was a rich country; they had plentiful natural resources. Oil most of all: the curse for development, the mother of conflict. They also had diamonds, *bloody diamonds and resources. Who owns them, the people or their masters? Who decides the fate of the bloody oil and diamonds? To hell with those resources! Do my people know what is being taken from the ground? The ground is rich. The ground is the source of life. My people have none of that! If they are left with anything it is useless and empty. I lament and I cry for my people. I weep, I weep, and I weep. I have never seen any of the local diamond miners' wives with diamonds on their fingers. Have you seen them with any of those fat stones? None of those people I know who go underground every day, who dig the ground, wear diamonds. Why? My own mother wore diamonds as if it was normal everyday jewellery, yet she never knew the location of a diamond or gold mine. Yet the women, the children and men who burrow for the diamonds may never own any.*

The people who knew where the mines were and understood the realities of mines were widows like Mamie Murphy. Her husband had been buried underground in a mine accident when he was on duty. The body was never brought to surface. There was no compensation. She had to sell fruits to support her and their six children. As a widow, though only in her forties, she resigned herself to a life of poverty. Remarriage was not an option. No one would touch a widow. Actually, take her as a wife officially. Though they secretly fathered children with the widows. Widows often magically became pregnant yet had no husbands. The odds were even more stacked against Mamie Murphy's children. The punitive cultures against widows, patriarchal structures strengthened by economic and large financial institutions, formed a solid base for inequalities.

Sahara arrived in Australia as a refugee under the Humanitarian Programme. She was also skilled refugee. Post resettlement, Sahara struggled to find meaningful work that matched her skills and credentials. So, she enrolled in yet another degree.

Sahara had changed jobs eight times in three years. She would say, 'I think I should be awarded a doctorate for being the most sacked, or job changer.' Between jobs, Sahara supported human rights causes. Her new Sociology degree, and her previous Law and Accounting degrees came handy.

After every job loss, Sahara would confide in Mumene, Afrika and Veronique. What vexed her were the shared experiences. When they met other friends, the stories and experiences were not too dissimilar. They all loved work, were eager to make a contribution, were punctual, and respectful, and even dropped down a few levels of qualifications to secure employment and support their families. They struggled to understand what they were doing wrong. They were apprehensive to speak openly outside their close group about their experiences.

They wondered how deeply rooted the problem was.

While on the phone during one of their many long conversations, Veronique recounted an experience to Sahara. In a shaky and distressed voice, she began, 'I walked in and greeted the lady at the desk, she responded with lips stretched as if she was smiling. Nothing else on her face moved. Was that a smile or a lip and cheek stretch? I'm used to the lip and cheek stretch, which I also know is a fake smile. It did not bother me. I took a sit next to a blonde beautiful girl. She seemed sweet but talkative. In the fifteen minutes we sat waiting, I could easily write her biography. She had applied for the office clerk role. She was surprised I had two Masters degrees. She even said she was surprised people like me would study that much. I did not respond. She then told me she had completed year twelve and planned to someday do a diploma course at TAFE. University, she said was not her thing. She was quite relieved when I told her I was not competing for the same office clerk role. As she chatted away, another lady walked up to us. I would find out later that she was the director of human resources and the interviewer as we settled in the interview room later.

She walked up, greeted us interviewees with kind eyes, and motioned to the other lady to follow her, no questions asked. She obeyed and followed. Moments later she returned and in an apologetic voice said, 'I had assumed you applied for the office clerk role, I am sorry, come with me,' I followed her. To finish, Sahara, I thought I did well at the interview. The feedback from all three panellists was excellent. I left confident. I never heard back. Not even one of those regretful letters has come to me.'

At that point in the conversation Veronique started sobbing, between tears she asked questions.

'What made her think that I was there for the office clerk role? Two of us were there, one white and one black. She could have just called us by name. I'm done with applications Sahara.'

As Sahara listened to Veronique, her own feelings of rejection resurfaced. Were such feelings justified? There was a valid story for every job change, especially the last job as a teacher aide.

CHAPTER 7

Teacher aide

'Sahara, welcome to our school, we are lucky to have you here. With all your skills we know you will make a good contribution to our pupils' lives. You have been assigned to one of the grade two classes. We have a young graduate there and she is struggling a bit with some of the students. You will be the aide for that class. She will however be your mentor during your probation time.'

'I thought you just said she was a graduate, Madam Principal, how can she mentor me?'

'Sahara, you've been instructed, and she will be good for you. We have some children who look like you, so we thought we should bring in someone from your country.'

'They may look like me but they may be from another country? Do you happen to know what country they have come from?'

'Africa, they are from Africa. You must speak the same language.'

'Madam Principal, Africa is a vast land. We have fifty- five countries. Thousands of dialects and languages.' With a smile Sahara added, 'do you know about the country of Europe and what language they speak?' At that point the principal's assistant knocked on the door to remind the principal of the next meeting and to help take Sahara to the grade two classroom.

Sahara was led by the principal's assistant and introduced to Miss. That was her introduction to the school and how things were done.

Miss was in fact a young graduate trying to find her feet. This was her first teaching position and she was in her second year as a teacher. Now she doubled as Sahara's mentor and supervisor 'as per the Position Description.'

Sahara found herself telling her 'mentor' how to manage the second grade, a group of seven-year olds who were all so cute but behaved like other seven-year-olds trying to affirm their place in their environment.

There were the triplets, who were somewhat new to the school. Unlike most of their classmates who had started in the preparatory grade, these triplets had joined in second grade after their parents moved from another state to be close to extended family. The triplets, new and trying to find their place within the established friendship groups, had brought tears to their Miss's eyes the last few weeks. Miss was young and bright but had really had little exposure with young kids outside her teaching placements. Miss loved teaching. She saw it as her calling, but now questioned her capabilities with these three. Yes, they were cute but not when it came to following instructions. They would all call out to 'Miiisssss' simultaneously, make the same requests together, and smile or shut their eyes at the same time. Miss was confused but did not want to call any attention to herself from the Madam Principal, Mrs Jacques-Douglas, or simply the 'The Doug' as she was commonly referred to. Miss just wanted to be a good teacher and keep her head down and please The Doug.

Sahara had a warm welcome from the young teacher. For two days Sahara did not utter a word to the kids or to the class teacher. Sahara sat quietly in a corner and observed in silence. One would not even know she was there. Then on her third day, Miss asked a question.

'Wait, wait, sit down you two.' Miss said softly as she gestured to two of the children to sit down.

'I Miiissssss', three little hands had sprung up at the same time.

'Yes Tam.' But before Miss could finish the sentence, Lam and Ting were interrupting.

'Okay Lam, Tam and Ting; I asked Tam not all three of you'

'But Miss, Mum said we have to do things together, she said we should be best friends. Ask Tam and Ting.'

'Yes Miissss, mum said so. That we should help each other in school,' Tam and Ting added.

'And Miiissssss, ...' came three voices.

'Okay children, we need to STOP now and listen. Miss asked Lam alone to respond. Lam alone, not all three of you, will speak.' Sahara stepped in. There was immediate silence and Tam finally had a chance to respond. Miss was surprised by the obedience of the children, smiled at Sahara in affirmation. It was a thumbs-up moment.

It was not the first time today that Ting, Lam and Tam all wanted to respond at the same time. Sahara had observed them interrupt, laugh and use their 'sibling power' together. She wondered why they were not in separate classes. But following conversations with Miss, Sahara realised no one there questioned The Doug's decision. It had been her decision to have all three together. The Doug was in charge everyone knew that.

Miss and Sahara worked together but were not close. After being together for some three months, neither could tell you anything about the other's life outside of work. Even the basic things like, single, or married, or have children had not been shared. They seldom shared family stories or anything about their private lives with each other. Though from two different continents, they were both obviously migrants, each brought with them a strong will to succeed.

The two were different, but their skills complemented each other. One was extroverted, the other introverted, or simply shy due to her upbringing. Both came from cultures that expected girls to listen without question, to obey and to follow, yet were now expected to lead. Sahara always questioned this logic.

Sahara, as the teacher aide, also supported the students who spoke English as a second language; it was sometimes their third or even fourth language. These children knew their numbers; they loved maths and science. They were sometimes unable to express themselves well in English but were maths prodigies. These kids often took language and maths classes over the weekends. Sahara, a numbers nerd, loved them, but also understood the family's push from new migrants for their children to succeed.

After the recent incident with the triplets, Miss was intrigued by how Sahara stopped them playing up almost instantly, but also by how they listened to her so attentively.

'Why do they listen to you and not me Sahara? I mean those three?'

'I am resolute with them?'

'I am too.'

'Are you?'

'I think so.'

'Can I ask a personal question? Can I?' 'Ask me anything. Permission given.'

'Thank you; do you have children of your own? Have you had much to do with kids, maybe nieces and nephews?

'Not really, I am an only child and my mum was an only child and since we moved here to Australia I have had little to do with children. Nothing really. But I love kids. I may have a child of my own one day. But those three don't make it desirable I must say.'

'I think you are treating them just like your mum treated you, her only child. That was probably how her mother did to her too. Think about it.'

'You are not the first to say that. My grandmother said the same and was quite worried that I was going to be a teacher in primary school. They always wanted me to be a doctor, a lawyer or an engineer'.

'That sounds like my family; actually, like my people. The children only have three professions to choose from: Doctor, Lawyer or Engineer. Outside of that, you are a FAILURE.'

'It may seem harsh but it's true. I completed a degree in accounting that I liked but went back and did law for my parents.'

'So, are these people all the same?'

'I am afraid so, it seems to me. It's not uncommon that the children do one degree for the parents and then one for themselves at some point. I mean, what they actually want. I did it the other way around. I had to.'

'Do you have children, Sahara?'

'I have two sets of twins at home, a set of three-year-old girls and seven-year-old boys. They attend another school close to home. It is a very good public school. I could never afford the private tuition here.'

'I am happy for you and the children, but I can understand about the tuition.'

Sahara wished her children could attend this school, but her income was 'not nearly enough'. She tried to convince The Doug that *Ahbotta* would pay. But it fell on deaf ears.

There was no winning. There was always a 'valid' rationale. She was a teacher aide.

Private education: if my children cannot do now, I will ensure my grandchildren and future generations are able to,

Sahara thought to herself. Her parents had dreamt about her future; she was now dreaming about that of her children. *How the world goes around.* Sahara sighed at this thought.

Sahara was raised to believe that you never wished anyone ill faith. God despises those who hate his children, and we are all God's children created in his very own image, something she was reminded of every week in Sunday school at her local church. Her maternal grandfather had served as the local catechist, and her mother instilled the values of the catechist's daughter into Sahara: a life of faith, prayer and devotion. Going to the nunnery was not too far from Sahara's mind until she met Johnny. He changed her world, and so did his mother. It's this faith and hope that Sahara believes has kept her alive all these years. Sahara thought the only reason she could withstand the many trajectories and protracted situations in her life were due to her faith; faith gave her inner strength and the capacity to overcome whatever storms came her way.

Here she was teaching in a private institution in a first world country yet could not afford the tuition there for her own children. Sahara saw her current situation as a time of trials. During such times, one's faith was tested, and if you are weak, the devil will control your mind. *"An Idle mind is a devil's workshop,"* she had been taught in Sunday school.

Sahara, a catechist's granddaughter, was never going to let herself fail, or let the devil into her house, or fall into his trap. Instead she would uphold the values that were instilled into her during doctrine classes. Never be covetous of anybody, let alone of innocent children whose earthly possessions they have no control of. These children live in a capitalist world surrounded by consumer parents, ever ready to pay for the next item. *Aren't we all victims of capitalism? If you are not, you must be an extraordinary being because many of us fall into the temptations of consumerism. Myself, Sahara included.* Check the abdominal circumference of the population to understand how capitalism affects us, especially the poorest of our society.

Unfortunately, like most other 'conditions', the poor are most affected by obesity. It is at such moments that Sahara would go down on her knees and recite the Lord 's Prayer quietly to herself. She would pray for God to give her and her family good health, for her community, and even for The Doug.

By the time she was through with prayers, tears streamed down her cheeks. Luckily these moments do not last long, though they have been more frequent in recent weeks.

Once over, Sahara would gather herself and face up to the next day again. That's exactly what she did next. Walked up to her pupils and did just what was expected of her; gave them the support they needed, instead of feeling sorry for herself. Sahara would embrace the pupils and give them whatever start their families dreamt for them and could afford to pay. The unmeasurable gift of hugs and love was what she cherished most and 'dispensed' to the pupils. Sahara thought of these hugs as a celebration of her motherhood and a gift for all children. These children were after all like hers. Sahara hoped someone was doing similar for her children where they were at school.

At this private school, across the staff cohort no one else looked like or sounded like Sahara. *But wasn't this multicultural Australia?* Sahara thought. *Were there artificial or imaginary boundaries to diversity that she was unaware of?* Sahara was forging her own path in life and wanted to take others along.

Sahara would ensure that the triplets focused on their work. *They are good kids, but they need a bit of firmness.* Sahara knew just what to say that made this trio sit still and focus.

As Sahara sat at lunchtime chatting with some of the pupils, Miss walked over to them. So introverted was she that she never said anything outside of class to Sahara, let alone exchange words beyond the polite greetings.

'Oh Sahara, do you have time for a cup of tea in the tearoom after classes today? Or we could also meet at the coffee shop across the street from the school tomorrow instead.'

'Hmmm, I need to get home for music lessons at 5:30pm. Okay, lets meet at the tearoom at 3:30pm for half an hour.'

'Sounds good to me, see you there.'

As the school day drew to an end, both women anticipated their first 'social event' together.

'Hello Sandy, you are here already?' Sahara greeted Miss by her first name.

'Just got here. What would you like? I was about to make myself a cup of peppermint tea.'

'I fancy a peppermint or camomile tea at this time of the day. Thank you. Err, no, on second thought I will have a coffee. Need the afternoon caffeine for the second shift at home with the boys.' Sahara quickly changed her mind as she smiled.

'How do you like it, white, sugar?'

'A short black, with half a teaspoon of sugar please.'

'There is a nice sofa in the corner, let's sit there,' Sandy said as she pointed to the sofa.

As the two women settled into their seats, they looked at each other but neither said a word for about thirty seconds, until Sahara broke the silence.

'Thanks for the coffee, Sandy. I certainly needed it.'

'After the days we've had, we both do.'

They spoke about the pupils, and they shared strategies to manage them when they are unruly. They discussed how to work on the strengths of their pupils and the decisions were agreed. Then the topic changed.

'Now that we have discussed work, do you mind if I ask a few personal questions so we can get to know each other even better Sandy?

'No, why not?' replied Sandy

'So, tell me, what brought you here, I mean to Australia?'

'My parents divorced, so with the stigma against single mothers back home, my mother thought Australia would give us a new beginning. It did too. I was only one at the time.'

'Interesting. So, you grew up here. Have you been back?'

'Not really, Mum never wanted to go back there. So, my grandma joined us after my grandpa passed on.'

'I'm sorry to hear that. So, three of you live together?'

'No, two of us, grandma and I. Mum passed away three years ago. She had bowel cancer. It was quick.'

Sandy became tearful as she spoke emotionally about her mother and the new life she had forged for their small family.

'Here, take, have some tissues.' Sahara said as she handed over a box of tissues to Sandy. She turned and gave Sandy a hug. 'These things do happen. My story is different, but not too far off yours. Will share when we next sit down for another coffee or tea together.'

'Thank you, Sahara; I did not realise how fresh this was in my mind. I miss my mother. She gave me everything any mother could, with the little she had. She left me financially secured. Aside from my teaching degree, I am a Petrochemical Engineer.' As Sandy mentioned the word 'engineer' both women chuckled between the tears and emotions.

'Was engineering your mother's degree and teaching yours?'

'Could not be said any better, Sahara. I did engineering for her and for grandma, and teaching for me. I also play the piano, very well too.'

'Such a talented young lady eh?'

'Sahara! You are so kind!'

'Sandy, I am only human.

'I admire your steadiness Sahara.'

'Ting, Tam and Lam; they are children just like mine. But they have been over loved. I show them love but have to help them on the straight path. That's why we are here. Enable them to become better citizens.'

'You bring in not only support staff skills. I notice you help the children with their maths and science sometimes. So what grade did you leave school?'

'Grade?'

'Yes, Grade 10, 11 or 12?'

Sahara looked at Sandy with questioning eyes, head tilted on the side briefly before responding. *Did I understand the question?* She thought to herself.

'Oh, I did not finish grades; I have two Masters degrees, one in accounting and the other in law; a degree for my parents and one for me. Recently I completed a Sociology degree.'

'Really?'

'Really.'

'No one mentioned that to me when you started. I thought … eemmm.'

Feeling uncomfortable, both women sipped their drinks. There was a moment of silence. They both stared at the notice board across the room from where they sat. Then Sahara looked at her watch, it was nearly 4:30 pm.

'Sandy, I am sorry but the time is running away from us. I must run off, else my children will be late for their music lessons. But it was nice to catch up.'

Sahara completed her sentence while on her feet. She put the cup into the dishwasher before making an exit.

'See you tomorrow, I mean on Monday, Sahara.'

'See you on Monday, Sandy. Thank you for the time and for sharing a personal story.'

The Doug walked in just as Sahara was about to leave room. She had heard her last sentence to Sandy: 'Thank you for the time and for sharing a personal story.'

'Good day Madam Douglas,' Sahara stopped briefly to greet her principal.

'Hello. You are still here at this time? Savannah?'

'Sahara,' She responded courteously with a sly smile.

'I'm sorry; the name is Sahara, not Savannah? But what's the difference? All African right?' Sahara strategically ignored the second question.

'We thought we'd get to know each other, so Sandy and I had tea and coffee after school. I'm sorry, but I must head off for the children's music lessons. Have a nice weekend Madam Douglas.'

At the mention of Sandy, The Doug turned and stared fiercely at Sandy. She did not even hear

Sahara finish her sentence. Sahara hurried out so the children were not late.

'Good afternoon Madam Douglas,' Sandy greeted.

'What are you two doing in here? Talking about me? I know you all dislike me being the principal here.'

'Err, nope. Just getting to know each other.'

'I shall get to the bottom of it. You are a member of the teaching staff; she is an Aide here at the school. Do you understand?'

'Yes, Ms Douglas. It's not what you are thinking.'

The two women continued the conversation in this way; The Doug using the opportunity to interrogate Sandy about Sahara.

Sahara was long gone. She had a good day and now she and Miss were beginning to bond. She had come to the end of her probation period.

Sahara left work that Friday feeling elated. She had finished another interesting week. She and Miss had had a good discussion on strategies to engage the pupils, without Miss getting frustrated by their endless calls and interruptions. Miss had appreciated the suggestions, she told Sahara.

As Sahara walked to her car she reflected on the day's events. There was a slight breeze, *which takes away any negative thoughts anyone may have,* she smiled as she hurried to her car. Her car was parked a few hundred metres away. She could not park on campus as she was on probation, so it was a walk away. She did not mind. *Exercise is good for you and for me.* Sahara walked briskly towards her car as she foraged for her car keys inside her bag. Today was also the last day of her probation period. *I think I have done well so far. Glad Sandy and I had that time together too. Poor girl, she lost her mother so young.*

Sahara was waiting for a confirmation letter for the teacher aide position. It was not the job she had hoped to do after all those studies, but at least it will keep her active while she waited for the right position. *I will never go on social security. I will do whatever it takes at this job so I can keep myself away from benefits. Those benefits are poverty maintenance, they keep you poor. You become just a name in the system.*

Meanwhile, Sahara had applied for another position at the same school as their financial officer. Accounts and numbers were her thing. She did well in the interview, she had been told.

Her pupils loved her here, and Sahara was beginning to know the people too. The Doug had even remarked about the differences she made in the classroom' some weeks earlier. The Doug was impressed with her performance, a rarity for The Doug. Sahara appreciated the feedback from The Doug. Despite that last encounter Sahara had a positive feeling. She would either be confirmed as an ongoing teacher aide or even better, would get the financial officer position. *I am not bothered starting at the bottom.* Then she received the letter.

CHAPTER 8

The letter

On Monday morning Sahara heard a loud knock at the door. She had decided to get rid of her doorbell some months earlier as some kids in the neighbourhood made it a point to play a chase game by ringing people's doorbells then running away. These children would disappear into thin air before one reached the door. After more than a dozen times of this cat and mouse game, Sahara made the sensible decision to do away with the doorbell. This kept her sanity and prevented a squabble with neighbours. 'If one has all the physical strength but is always at loggerheads with their neighbours, they have to always look over their shoulders; they will not have peace.' Sahara did not want all the power with no peace, the reason for getting rid of her doorbell. All guests had to knock instead.

This particular Monday morning was quiet. Sahara was up early to prepare herself for work and get the children ready for school. She heard three knocks on the door. She went and opened the door; a gush of cold breeze swept past and hit her face. At the door was a tall gentleman standing by the doorway with a small envelope and machine in hand.

He had a thick red jacket for warmth on a cold winter morning.

'Good morning.'

'Good morning.'

'Ms Sahara?'

'Yes, Sahara.'

'Please sign here.' He said, pointing on the little electronic machine he had. She smiled at the courier man as she signed for the letter. The letter was handed over to Sahara. *It is hard to sign with those plastic sensors on another slippery plastic, let alone on a morning like this,* Sahara thought to herself. Today was particularly cold; her fingers almost froze as she stepped out of the door unto the porch. Still smiling, she thanked the *messenger*.

The courier man, she thought was the *post office messenger.* The exchanges had been quick. *Messengers have a lot of responsibility,* she thought.

Sahara's grandmother, *Yaya*, as she was affectionately known to all the grandchildren and in the community, always uttered protective words to her children before sending them on long errands through the village's narrow paths. These trails took one through the rolling knolls around the village and countryside. 'These wonderful knolls and peaks were testament to God's power,' Yaya would remind her family. The paths were full of stones and on cold mornings, especially during the harsh harmattan, putting a foot wrong or hitting a stone with bare feet would hurt. Even hitting a toe against a small pebble could hurt like hell. Yaya would say, *'if you hit your leg with a stone, let the stone break into two halves, not your foot,'* as she sent you out. It meant: let no harm nor danger come your way or befall you on this mission, be it by the doing of man or by the spirits of the hills; you will be safe. Before uttering such special 'blessings', Yaya would place her two open palms loosely on the child's temple over their ears and would symbolically spit three times on their forehead. Sahara had wondered, as she closed the door behind the courier, whether his grandmother had performed a similar ritual before 'sending' him on this errand.

Those symbolic blessings from Yaya's home had been superseded with financial incentives, Sahara thought. Sahara quickly tried to eliminate such thoughts from her mind, and to instead focus on the outing later in the day with her mother-in-law. More so, it was a letter, not the parcel from *Chique Boutique.* She could not deny or block her mind from the fact that it was cold, wet and windy. The gush of cold air had hit her in the face. It was a swift reminder of those dry cold harmattan mornings, and of Yaya's messages about how such mornings could bring bad luck to people. *There were those three knocks on the door. No bad luck.* So, there was no fear.

Sahara walked into the house and examined the envelope carefully. She smiled, then placed it on the table next to the French vase that was holding half a dozen fresh white roses. She wanted to open the envelope but was hesitant. Instead she went into the kitchen and made herself a cup of coffee, her morning routine. There was the nice coffee machine in cream white and yellow, another of Johnny's presents, but Sahara opted for the old clay coffee pot for her coffee today. It will boil while she read the letter. *My confirmation letter or the new position,* she wondered.

Sahara sat on a chair next to the dining table. It was a sizeable dining room with beautiful French and Italian décor. There were African artefacts at various points in this room. Johnny considered himself a 'collector', and with what he had, it would make a great heirloom for his family and future generations.

There was a large wooden pot, almost six-feet-tall, with a diameter of about 30cm. The inside was hollow, and the outside had several 'faces'. This 'fetish' pot would have seen many a 'barren' woman over the years, visiting its owner somewhere in far West Africa as they sought fertility medicine. Looking at the pot, one would say it had seen its day. It was over a century old and would live for many more human lifetimes. *I wish us humans could have the lifespan of trees. Some species live for centuries, or even millennia, yet never go out daily chasing money. Money rules us yet does not speak to anyone of us. Sitting next to someone, you never know how much of it he or she has in his or her account. Money, money, money; who made it, and how did it take over us?* Sahara wondered how the medicine pot found itself in Australia.

Sahara settled down on the leather chair with her cup of coffee in hand. The lounge suite was another mother-in-law gift. Sahara took a few sips of her coffee from the *Vero Gann* mug that Afrika gave her as a birthday present. Sahara liked *fabulous*, and 'fabulous' was her middle name to friends. She loved the fine things in life, reminiscent of her life before the war back home. She took a gold-plated letter opener and slowly but steadily opened the letter from the school. With a smile, she looked forward to reading it. *This is not the harmattan, this is Australia; it must be good luck. Those three knocks must be luck.*

Sahara hoped she had been offered her current position on an ongoing basis, or better still, the new position she applied for as the financial administrator. After all she was a trained accountant. As Sahara began to read the letter, tears began to roll down her cheeks. She was grief stricken. She wept quietly, as streams of tears gushed down her cheeks. Sahara could be emotional, especially when there was good news. *Was it good news, or had her grandmother's words simply come to fruition?* The letter read:

1st of January 2017 10/11 Walker Avenue, South Melbourne, Victoria, 3001.

Dear Sahara,

This letter confirms the end of your probation period. We thank you for your service to our school community. The students loved your presence and you have good potential.

The class teacher, who served as your supervisor and mentor, provided us with feedback about your time with her. We hope this will help you as you continue your search for employment.

Based on that report, we concluded that you were burdened by the children and found it difficult to settle them, especially the new students. Your mentor's efforts to support you were not well received by yourself. She felt some training in children's services might enhance your development and develop the skills required for this Teacher's Aide role.

Our school community appreciates the time you spent with us and we wish you all the best in your future endeavours.

Sincerely,
Martina Jacques-Douglas Principal.

After reading the letter, many thoughts stampeded through Sahara's mind. Not only was this unexpected; she knew *'you never shoot the messenger.'* She had signed for this letter from the *messenger* herself; if only she had known the letter's contents. Sahara was punctual, knowledgeable, courteous, and had good communication skills. She was opinionated; *who isn't?* Sahara encouraged her students to have opinions. She shared her ideas with them, as well as at staff meetings. She had been encouraged to do this from a young age at school.

I was the Aide and she was the Teacher. But we had separate roles. Maybe Sahara was, as she was advised at another time, 'uncontrollable'. But how do you define 'uncontrollable' and 'submissive'? Didn't women fight for the right to voice their opinions for centuries? We're supposed to have these rights today, yet we're not allowed to use them! The chains of control and submissiveness remain! What was it, I did not communicate about?

And 'loud': what does that mean? Must everyone be subdued? Only smile with our teeth rather than from our heart? We're supposed to sing from the same hymnbook about celebrating difference. Is there only one type of 'difference', or 'difference' for only one type of people? Should we all conform and behave the same? Is individuality not what we all proclaim? What diversity, what gender gaps are we closing? And … I cleaned chicken feet with an accounting degree! I was fired for writing too detailed reports, potentially 'exposing' the company to litigation if their accounts were audited. While the words in this letter may be different, there was a common undertone: *'Need more development, more skills.'*

She opted not to say anything at this time to Ahbotta but needed an excuse for not going to work that day.

Sahara instead turned to her support team; she called Afrika and Veronique. They consoled her but reminded her that she must not give up. Afrika's words were precise: *You decided to go too low, that's what happens. You become a threat if you are over-qualified. The right role will come at the right time, Sahara. Think about me, Sahara, and all of the applications that I submitted.*

Afrika at one point had tried being a translator as she was a native French speaker, spoke two other local dialects, and was now fluent in English. She was a quick learner and nothing was too difficult for her to learn. She still 'failed'.

'Thank you, Afrika, and thank you Veronique. Please let Mumene know if you get hold of her before me.'

Sahara's grandmother's words ran through her mind as she sat there. 'Sahara, make use of your opportunities; do your best. Take initiative and help when needed. Do your best every day, wherever you are. Safe journey my child, I shall see you when you come back. Go well my child.' Those were her grandmother's words at her home many years ago during one of the family visits. Those words have stayed with her and she took them everywhere.

Were these traits now suddenly a weakness? Were they a weakness for others, or for some only?

As tears rolled down Sahara's cheeks, she wondered about Mumene. Before she could go to share the news with Johnny, she heard one of the four children call out. She dried her tears, then picked *Fonnwi* up. They had a long warm cuddle, another dawn for this mother. As she cuddled her daughter, the others filed in and ran straight into her arms. She was a good mum and they loved her warmth.

Innocently, they gave her a big hug; it brought joy, 'dried the tears of hurt' from Sahara's eyes and heart. The children had no idea what had just happened. She smiled at all four and thanked her God for another day.

'Now go back upstairs and I will join you shortly,' she instructed the children after their group hug. They obeyed without question. *Had they sensed anything? Children can have magical powers.*

Sahara, now even more determined, refused to grieve. Her thoughts turned to *Mumene* again: *I will call her later.* She could confide in any of them. They were close. More like sisters than friends brought together by their parents in a strange way. Rejection hurts, but true friends and family last forever. They will always provide you with warmth. Sahara often thought of friends and other people with similar stories.

After all her trials and job hunting and firings, Afrika had finally secured a job in her area of expertise with a mining firm. Her boss had travelled the world, and he focused on talent and nothing but talent. If anything, he hired more migrants and second-generation workers in his firms. He loved seeing women lead. *'I know women are good leaders; if they've managed homes for millennia, they can manage anything,'* he often reminded himself.

CHAPTER 9

Johnny, Ahbotta's son

The Wise woman, who had been ostracised until the missionaries arrived in her town, was kind-hearted. She was never fazed by the many rumours of her *eating children*. Considered a witch, she had lived an almost isolated life, interacting with the wider community only when she had to. She was comfortable. She had inherited her parents' wealth and had land in her name, a rarity for women back then. Maybe that's why she was ostracised.

Johnny was one of her seven 'rescued' children. Johnny had a very rich first year of life, full of joy until war in his parents' own country and their subsequent deaths. Johnny had been handed to 'mother' for 'treatment' by his maternal grandmother. Johnny's frail maternal grandmother could no longer care for him after his parents' demise. He was an AIDS orphan but was unlike other orphans. Unknown to this 'new mother', Johnny was an heir. Rather than let Johnny waste to death as she was also frail, his grandmother, as a last option in her search for treatment and care for her grandson, handed him to the Wise woman to try any 'medicine' that would keep him alive. When she traced and found the Wise woman, she recounted her misfortune and the loss of her only daughter.

'I have lost everything already. My only daughter is gone. This one child, I have tried. Do what you can. God will show you the way and open your eyes and his. Bring him back to me when you can. But you can see, I am an old woman. I do not have long on this earth.' With those words, Johnny was handed to the Wise woman, now his 'new mother'; his grandmother left him there with her. She trusted a stranger with her only daughter's only child.

Johnny's maternal grandmother came from neighbouring Dach; she had traced her way to the Wise woman's town over two decades ago. That's how Johnny arrived at the Wise woman's household.

Mother raised him with the others. *Johnny was a blessing,* she would say; *the only son.* It was only when Johnny was about to marry that 'mother' told him his real-life story. She did the same for every one of her other children. Johnny was the last of them all.

Johnny loved 'mother', and never thought of any other mother. He had only ever known her as mother. Johnny also resigned himself to the tradition that any woman he would marry was also 'mother's wife'. Ahbotta's tradition was Johnny's too. Johnny loved mother, and always thought about the 'life' she had given him. But he sometimes wondered in what world his 'birth mother' had lived – the one she left decades ago – now he had a window into her life. He was the son of diplomats; but another mother, in another country where they were refugees, raised him.

As Johnny sat with his friends sharing stories about their mothers and the push to marry, he spoke about his mother for the first time to his closest friend; he opened up about his background.

'My mother is here physically, but mentally she is sometimes over there. I mean there in the country she left a long time ago. She seems to be in a time capsule.'

'Johnny, that is her world. That is what she knew. That is her reality.'

'You know, I'd also like to understand about my other world. The family I was born into. All I know about my heritage is what 'mother' told me. I was born in Temen where my father was an Ambassador; 'mother' found that out. My family had returned to my parents' country of birth – Dach – when I was only six months old for a family visit. The plan had been to visit biannually, so I could stay connected with the extended family in Dach. War broke out while we were in Dach. The new military government cancelled all diplomatic passports and froze all the diplomats' bank accounts. It was swift.

My parents apparently had been on antiretroviral drugs that were no longer accessible or affordable when the war broke out. They couldn't get their basic vitamins too. My mother was strict and had adhered to treatment while pregnant, so I was born without the virus. But no one knew my parents had contracted the disease; that they had HIV.

Back then, the stigma associated with the disease killed people first, before the illness did. Not even the virus killed as many people as the psychology of knowing they were HIV positive and the ostracising that ensued. Both my parents, I learnt, were dead within six months of arriving in Dach. Their deaths were two months apart, to be precise. I was only a year old then, I would later learn. I was their only child.

My parents were wealthy, but my poor grandmother had little knowledge about their wealth and where their money was. Even if she knew, she would not have been able to protect anything. The new regime cut a swathe through everything and everyone linked to the previous government. Rumours, I heard, were enough for them to get rid of you.

My grandmother was shattered. Her only daughter was now dead. My grandmother thought the illness that these parents had died from could affect me. She also thought they may have been poisoned and was scared that the same people will come after their child. She was old and becoming frail. She wanted to rescue me, but with the instability, things quickly deteriorated. She feared for my health and survival, I was told.'

Head bowed, Johnny's eyes welled and he fought back tears. His friend held Johnny's hand gently but firmly, and with her left hand raised his chin, pulled him to herself and gave him a long passionate kiss.

Johnny responded affectionately. Until this moment they were just friends.

Slowly, she pulled herself away. Still holding Johnny's hand, she asked him, 'What else did 'mother' say about your parents and grandmother?'

'Grandmother knew her daughter had friends of status like her and her husband, but she had no way of tracing anyone with war and chaos all over the place. Had things been normal, she could go to the embassy and speak to the *big people*. Once the war broke, the *big people* took what they could from the State coffers. People disappeared, money disappeared; so, did the society and those systems that took centuries to build. It all disappeared with them too. It was *everyone for themselves and God for us all*. You focused on you and nothing else. People ran from the cities to the villages. Men disguised themselves in women's attire, to increase their chances of survival. Children ran and left their mothers behind when they heard armies approaching their towns and villages. Mothers encouraged children to run and disperse in different directions to enhance their chance of surviving. At least this would assure that a soul could be saved to continue the family line, rather than all be killed in one setting if they were all together.

It must have been dreadful and terrifying just being there. But I am here. Not sure how I was saved.'

His friend's face was wet and as she sobbed silently in Johnny's hands while listening patiently to him.

'I am not finished yet. Now that I started, you deserve to know who I am and why I am here.'

Holding back tears, she nodded.

'My grandmother, mother later told me, had faith. Grandmother did not know my fate when she brought me to mother for 'treatment'. She had told mother that I was her only grandson and had barely survived. She did not know the sickness I had. I had no sickness, at least the one that killed her daughter and my father; I was frail and maybe I was hungry. I may have been malnourished when I think about it. Grandmother had heard of a Wise woman in neighbouring Kamaran, a stable place back then. She wanted to save her grandson, her only daughter's child.'

Tears rolled down his cheeks, his nose ran while he shared this story.

His friend was in tears by now too. They were both emotional. As she spoke in a shaky but soft voice, they also knew at this point that they were in love. Something had changed very suddenly.

'War, its burden and the lives that war destroys! What infuriates me, Johnny, is that these countries that are locked in these wars manufacture no weapons. So where do the weapons come from? Who pays for them? How do they pay for them? Who really benefits, Johnny?' Sorry to interrupt, but my heart aches.'

'I understand; can you imagine what it is like for me? My grandmother was good, mother told me. With the little money her daughter gave grandmother for her personal upkeep, it was those savings that saved us. With it, grandmother could afford to take me to 'mother' in a faraway land. Grandmother knew her daughter and her husband had money in the bank but had no access to it. She had never had a bank account of her own, so did not know what to do. She would have kept her money in 'secret' places, such as under her mattress or under banana trees outside, as people did back then.

Grandmother was to return in three months to pay the Wise woman, and hopefully to have a healthier grandson to take back home. Four years passed; no one heard from her. Mother wondered what had happened to her but had no means of tracing her. It was dangerous to do that and still is. She never returned. At age five, 'mother' officially adopted me. I became her son.

She had fostered other children, but she adopted me before the others, though I was the youngest of them all. Three years later, mother had to flee with me. We spent time in the *Samaku* refugee camp. I am sorry my dear. I did not realise how much this weighed on me. I was a refugee at one, and again at eight years of age, yet was born into a wealthy family. By the age of eight, I was fluent in Swahili, French, Arabic and Ngemba, but spoke no English. That was when we arrived in Australia. My family, with mother as the head, made a life and home here in Melbourne. Mother never looked back. This was her second relocation; it was the fourth for me, and I was only eight.'

There was a big sigh of relief from both Johnny and Statina. Johnny kissed Statina on the forehead. They buried themselves passionately into each other's arms. Johnny then turned slowly, picked her up and carried her into his room. They made love passionately.

Ahbotta had always been worried about Johnny not marrying a girl from among her people. Statina was always around. She was fond of her, but now it seemed she was taking her son and his heart away from his people.

Ahbotta always longed for Johnny to connect with his roots, especially his bloodline. She had a desire for Johnny to marry a girl from her hometown, to irreversibly cement his place in the hearts of the local people. Marrying their daughter would make her his and him theirs. Now with Statina always around, Ahbotta was worried yet determined. Johnny will go home and marry among her people. She will plan the trip and will pay for it. Ahbotta was getting apprehensive about the future bride. *She does not look like us, she acts differently, can't cook our food. Not a wife for Johnny. She is a good child, but not a wife.*

She is like a broomstick. Those thoughts were never far from Ahbotta's mind. *Cultural week activities at home used to provide perfect opportunities for youth and students to mingle during summer holidays. That's when he should go.*

Over the next few weeks, Ahbotta would pester Johnny about the trip back to Africa.

'Johnny did you consider the trip as we discussed?'

'Mother, those people don't know me and I do not know them. Is this your strategy to punish me?'

'Punish you? Why?'

'Well, why are you sending me there?' 'Johnny, you'll understand when you grow up.'

'Mother, I am an adult, what do you mean by grow up?'

'My son, you are always a child while your parents are alive.'

With a stern look and an exasperated grunt, Johnny turned his back, and as he walked away, he replied to his mother:

'Mother, just do what you want to do! Just tell me and I'll do it! Pay the tickets and I'll go! I shall also try to find some information about my father, as you said before.'

'Now you are beginning to reason like a man, like my son. May you live long to see the great grandchildren.'

'Great grandchildren … I have no children yet! I don't even have a wife, I don't even know if I want one!'

'Johnny, what man among our people refuses to take a beautiful woman and continue the family bloodline?'

'Mother, is that the only reason you marry? To make more children and populate the world?'

'Why else would you want to marry? You have become so selfish my son; you are forgetting the ways of our people.' On that note Johnny turned around to face his mother again. 'OK mother, what if I marry? When do you want that to happen? Do you have the woman I have to marry already?

Tell me. I'm tired of being an only child, an only son! Truly I am!'

'Son, I know the type of woman, but I do not have her yet. She is tall, black with a round bosom with strong hips, that is a good sign that she will bear children, many children Johnny. When you go, keep those big eyes wide open. I shall keep my ears open for the news.'

Shaking his head, Johnny was done with this; he slammed the door behind him and went straight into bedroom where he walked in and slammed the door behind him as well. He lay on his bed and wept. His mind returned to Statina. *I love her but my mother and family will never accept her. She will live in misery. I can't put her through such pain.*

Johnny's mother, on the other hand, smiled and walked away after this discussion. That was how Statina came to be obliterated from Johnny's life. That was a year, before Johnny's big trip.

Mother organised the tickets, and within weeks, Johnny was back in Kamaran with Ahbotta's people. He also travelled to his grandmother's country.

Johnny was back with his mother's people, whom he considered his people too. His mother was determined for him to have a cultural exchange. Johnny was also keen to fulfil his mother's wish to find a wife among her people.

Johnny would later travel to spend three weeks with mother's people while he learnt about his identity.

CHAPTER 10

The home coming

As Johnny sat with his new friends, a young woman who looked confused walked up to them. This was the second person in the last hour. He and a group of lads and ladies were drinking locally brewed beer. Johnny does not remember drinking palm wine before but took to it once he tasted it. His friends ordered wine and western beer; he ordered palm wine. His friends were perplexed: Why would you prefer palm wine to red wine? *Well,* Johnny would respond, 'wine is wine,' as he shrugged his shoulders.

The young lady walked up to them; she looked confused but had a certain confidence in her voice.

'*Bonjour*, excuse me! Sorry to interrupt your conversation but I am trying to find an old building on *'Avenue de Cadre'*. The building had three shops in front of it, but I do not seem to be able to locate it.'

The gentlemen and the two ladies looked at each other, somewhat puzzled. 'What are you looking for?' asked one of the women.

'A large building with three shops.'

'We don't speak English,' responded another of the ladies in broken English, with a French accent.

As the women engaged in conversation, the men simply stared at Sahara. One almost caught a fly in his mouth, it was so wide open.

'*Quelle Beauté!*' ('*What a beauty!*') said one of the men, his eyes fixed on Sahara's bosom.

'*Quoi?*' ('What?') said the other, almost shaken by the response. The response was directed at his friend, who was staring at Sahara from the side.

One of the men sprang to his feet and responded.

'You can speak to me in English or French or Swahili, Mademoiselle.'

'Your English is definitely good, sir.' '

Where is that accent from?'

'I'm visiting from the UK and am trying to locate a few family and other things. Been away for a while. It's a bit hard when no one uses street names, even when they are there. Someone told me to walk until I turn right, and when I see a big mango tree, I should continue straight on for about five minutes until I come to a bar that is painted red on the outside. He said that the locals drink there and there will surely be someone there to assist me.'

Why wouldn't they just use the street names? Did they even know that the street names were there? Sahara pondered.

'I see,' one of gentlemen responded, as he sprang to his feet at the same time.

'Hello friends, I may have to help this lady to a place down the *quartier,* (quarter).'

'But ...' Before his friends could say anything, he turned and motioned to the young lady to follow him. He turned and led both of them away.

'Oh, I almost forgot to say I'll be back shortly. That's whenever I finish helping this beautiful ...'

He did not finish the sentence before his 'friends' burst into laughter. He smiled and walked away without another word spoken.

The young woman in need of help was hesitant after the reaction by the others, but she obliged. Time was against her on this mission, and she needed all the help she could get.

I'll have to take the risk, she thought.

As they walked away from the others into the quarter, the gentleman's attention returned to the young lady. His first impression of her was: *beautiful!*

'So how long are you here for?' he asked.

'My trip is almost coming to an end.'

'How long is coming to an end?'

'Three days, or 76 hours to be exact.'

'Okay, I see,' the gentleman nodded. They walked for a while with no words. He led the way while she followed about two steps behind.

Sahara finally broke the silence.

'So where is the place?'

'Hmmm, just follow me.'

They walked and walked until they came to a group sitting outside in a small shed close to a mansion. It was not dissimilar to other nearby buildings.

'Where are the shops?' She turned to him. She spoke softly but firmly.

'I'm about to ask these people?'

'What, I thought you knew where you were going!'

'To be honest, I have been here for two weeks and I have seen a few shops in the area you pointed at, but I need to be sure we are headed in the right direction.'

'Seriously, you just wasted another hour of my time?' It had been a long walk.

'I'm sorry, but this was my only opportunity to speak to you.'

'But you do not even know me!'

'I know that, I do not know you. But I would like to know you now!'

'What will you like to know? I need to go as my time is limited, and you know that already.'

'I want to know more.'

'Sorry', the beauty said as she turned to this new group of gentlemen sitting in the little hut. She spoke in French, but none of them seemed to understand.

Then the man who had walked with her this far intervened again.

'I can translate! Go on, speak in English, Arabic or Swahili.'

With a straight face, she obliged, and he translated.

The day ended with no results, and they found themselves more confused than when they met.

Just before they parted, he turned to her

'I am Johnny! And you?'

'I am Sahara.'

'Nice to meet you, beautiful ... Sahara. Has anyone ever told you how beautiful you look?'

'Nice to meet you, Mr Johnny. Thanks for the help, though it amounted to nothing.'

As she turned to walk in the opposite direction, Johnny turned to her and asked her if she wanted to walk back to where they had met.

'I need to go back to those friends. They might be still there waiting for me, as I invited them out and I need to go settle the bill.'

'Actually, I recognise this place; I walked past it a few days ago. It's only about fifteen minutes' walk from where I am staying. One of the new hotels down the main road from here.'

'Can I walk you back?'

'Not really, thank you for your help.'

As they parted, Johnny almost sprinted to where his friends were. They were still sitting there and they had not only been drinking, they also had some dinner.

'Johnny, you abandoned us. Did you lose your mind with that girl?' One of the lads taunted.

'Would you not? Man, I did not even know where I was going. We actually got lost, but I dared not let her know. I just wanted to walk with her.'

He took a seat next to one of the young ladies who threw her head on his shoulder immediately.

'Hello Johnny,' she said softly, with her head touching his head.

'Sorry Hilda, not here for that,' as he moved away from her.

'Can I have some more wine? I mean the type I drink that comes from the tall trees?' Johnny asked, directing his attention to the bar attendant. He drank his serve quickly before springing to his feet again.

'I must leave! I have some urgent business to attend to!

I almost forgot, and it's getting late.'

'You have hardly sat down Johnny,' replied Hilda.

'Madam, can you bring me the bill? Everything they have consumed.'

Johnny settled the bill. He was in such haste; the others were confused but no questions were asked. He had paid for their four rounds of drinks, so they were satisfied.

Johnny stopped the next taxi and asked the driver if he could hire his services for a couple of hours. The offer was too good to turn down. The taxi driver turned to all the other passengers in the car and politely told them to take other taxis. They did not need to worry about paying him. They obliged; they had no other choice. Those who were close by their destination simply walked the rest of the distance. Almost all did, but for one who had just boarded. It was a good deal for everyone. One of the passengers turned and said to another, *'he must be one of those Americana visitors.'* Actually, he sounded like an *Australiana.*

Johnny jumped into the cab. 'Can you take me to the new hotel down the road?' He tried to direct the driver, but because he had walked through the back streets rather than the main roads, he was not sure where the hotel was. He did not even know the name of the hotel. Luckily everyone here tends to be nosy.

'Are you staying there?'

'No, but I have a friend staying there, and we need to go out for dinner.'

'That place is expensive! A night can easily cost what I make in two weeks, sometimes three weeks if I don't meet someone like you.'

'Slow down, this is the area. Yes, that is the mansion where we spoke to the guys, and it should not be far from here.'

'I told you I know it, I will take you there, *Saar*'.

As they arrived, Johnny turned to the driver.

'Okay Mr. Driver; here is your money. You can wait here or you can come back in an hour, but I shall pay you now for the full two hours.'

'Two hours *Saar*, thank you,' the driver spoke as he took the money with both hands. There was also a tip, nearly half of what he had offered to pay him in the first place. The smile on the driver's face could not be erased.

Johnny adjusted his shirt and walked up to the receptionist. In French he greeted her and asked about a 'friend Sahara' who was staying there.

'No. There is no one here with that name.'

'Are you sure?'

'Yes, I am sure *Saar*.'

With a deep sigh, he turned to her and asked,

'Is this not the new hotel here?'

'Yes, this is new, but there is another one not far from here.'

'Do you know the name of the hotel?'

'No, *Saar*.'

'Thank you, bye.' Johnny said as he turned and walked out.

Johnny had been so carried away by the woman's beauty that he had forgotten to ask her basic information like the name of her hotel.

Confused and annoyed with himself, Johnny sat down on the couch in the lobby, hoping the driver would show up earlier than arranged. He looked at his watch at least half a dozen times every few minutes. He stood and paced up and down. Just as he was about to walk away, he noticed a familiar face.

'Hello, what are you doing here?' she asked.

'Err, I came, I came to err …'

'Johnny, are you staying here?'

'I thought I'd check if they have a room for me for the next few nights. The lady is checking and will confirm.'

'Are you sure?'

'Okay! I came to look for you, Sahara! I have been waiting for two hours.'

'I'm not staying here, Johnny. I am in another hotel not far from here. I came to check if I could stay my last two nights somewhere else, as I heard this is a nice place.'

'Madam, can you check if you have two spare rooms for the next two or three nights, please?'

'Two rooms? Are you sure? This place is different to other hotels here. It's very expensive. Only the rich people stay here. The ministers and their families and the rich business ladies and men.'

'Can you not lecture me about the inequalities here?

Just give me a two-bedroom suite or two separate rooms.' ''I am sorry *Saar*; I will check.'

'You are very lucky! We have the last two rooms, the *Suite Majestique.* It's one of our most expensive suites.' 'Confirmed!' Then, turning to her: 'Sahara, can you go and bring your luggage? I will do this? Or you can wait for me to help you. That taxi out there is for me. He can take you first.'

'No pressure Johnny, I can wait.'

The receptionist was surprised that he could afford the cost of such a suite. *That's my income for four weeks here,* she thought.

'That was quick. You must have been close by, Sahara'

'Indeed, I was only a few doors down the street. It was an ordinary place. This place is much better, Johnny. I decided to spend my last few nights here, to at least have some comfort in the middle of all the chaos. I mean good chaos.'

'So, can we take you to the *Suite Majestique?*'

'Yes, all good. And you? Will you be staying in the room next door?'

'It's a suite, Sahara. But don't be afraid, we have two separate rooms, and I am a perfect gentleman,' he said with a smile.

At that point he turned and walked towards the elevator.

'Sorry *Saar,* our lifts are not working. You may use the stairs instead. I am sorry madam,' the receptionist said as she turned to Sahara motioning her to follow.

'Please follow your husband.'

'He is not my husband; he is a … friend.'

'Sorry madam, follow your friend,' the receptionist said in a slightly sarcastic tone as she helped them with their luggage.

'Seriously, what does work in this place? How could a hotel like this not have a lift that works?' Knowing there was nothing she could do, and not wanting to ruin her evening, Sahara obliged.

'Leave the luggage behind. Someone will bring it to you.' 'Thank you, could that be soon?'

Sahara waited for a quarter of an hour for her luggage to arrive.

As Sahara unpacked her suitcase, Johnny did the same in the adjoining room. She walked into the bathroom to have a fresh shower.

Sahara saw two buckets filled with water in her bathroom! *Why water in buckets in a place like this?* Sahara undressed, walked to the bathroom then turned on the hot tap, but there was no water.

There is no water in this place? Seriously? OMG.

Unknown to her, Johnny was experiencing similar trouble in his room; no running water; only 'trickles'.

Frustrated Sahara called out to Johnny.

'Is your shower running Johnny?'

'Can't say it is running. There are trickles of water, I would say,' Johnny sighed. 'I thought this place was what they said it was, or at least what it looked like in reception.'

'May I come in there for the trickles? You at least have something coming out. I have nothing here. How do they expect us to pay such money and have no water to shower with?'

'I'm almost done. A few more minutes and you can come in.'

Following their 'showers', Sahara and Johnny shared a meal together in the restaurant.

'Thanks Johnny, you are so kind. I have to take a rest, as I will need to be up quite early.'

'Goodnight. Can I kiss you on the forehead, Sahara?' Johnny said as he lowered his head to do just that.

Sahara did not resist.

Johnny turned and left.

They both retired to their own rooms.

The alarm went off at 7am. Sahara turned, half asleep, and pressed the off button. It was another hour before she jumped out of bed when she heard a knock on the door.

'Sahara, I thought you wanted to leave early? It's 8am.

Are you ready? Let's have breakfast together.'

'I'm sorry, still in bed. Shall be ready in half an hour.

Sorry, I over slept.'

'Now sleeping beauty, get ready. I shall wait for you.'

Okay, I shall be as quick as I can.'

'Go on then.'

Sahara yawned and stretched, got out of bed, and rushed into the bathroom. She jumped into the shower. This time there was hot water, and the water pressure was right. She smiled. She began to sing in the shower; she did that most days when she was happy.

She joined Johnny in the shared sitting room where he sat. As the pair walked down the stairs, Johnny reached out his hand to hold Sahara's, but she pulled it away. He shrugged his shoulders and said nothing. Little was said over breakfast, until Sahara broke the silence.

'Are you going to help me today?'

'Do you need my help, Miss Independent?'

'I may, Mr Gentleman.'

'If you say so, I will.'

'Thank you! You are so kind. I hope we do not get lost today,' she said with an enigmatic smile.

'The only reason I'm here now is because we got lost yesterday. I also got lost finding where you were staying, and then as I was about to leave, in you walked. There is something to be said about being lost.'

'I thought you knew the neighbourhood. Don't you live here?'

'I know as much as you do, to be honest.'

'So, you lied to me?'

'How else could I have engaged someone like you in conversation?'

'Oh you ...'

'Say it! It's all right. Call me whatever you want.' Johnny's eyes were fixed on her as he spoke the words. 'Say it, Miss In...de...pen...dent.'

Sahara said no more. Instead she paused, and after a minute she looked at Johnny.

'Who are you and what are you doing here?'

'I'm on holidays from Australia. My mother sent me here to learn about my roots. It's complicated.'

'Not as complicated as mine; but I knew you were different. I had the gut feeling you were not a true local.'

Over the next two days, Johnny helped Sahara around. They both learnt a lot about each other over those two days, and they learnt even more about themselves.

Johnny had found out that some individuals were trying to trace 'a child and a woman who lived up in the hills'. The lady had children in her care at various times but had simply vanished. Johnny listened carefully. Contact details had been left with the town's chief and the local mayor. Johnny promised to follow the leads: *Maybe I could finally meet someone of my bloodline.* Johnny would return to Australia armed with that information.

Sahara was there on a personal mission too: to trace her father's disappearance and news of her mother's whereabouts. She and her siblings vowed to continue the search for their mother and for the cause of their father's death in custody. She had already been there for three weeks, and time was running out. She only had a few days before her flight back to London. She was more determined than ever to get some closure. With no smart phones or even telephones, Sahara was completely dependent on the generosity of the locals and friends. She got lost in an old district, where her parents had owned property.

The meeting with Johnny was nothing more than chance. At the end of the two days, the pair exchanged numbers. They promised to speak to each other once they got home.

But Johnny misplaced Sahara's number. He was mad at himself. How could he? He searched his wallet at least five times. Two months later his phone rang. Johnny recognised the voice on the phone instantly but wanted to be sure.

'Sahara?' Johnny's heart leapt with joy.

'Hi Johnny. You recognised my voice.'

'How could I forget?'

'Why did you not call?'

'I have been searching for your number. I was planning a trip to the UK to come trace you.'

'What? Really?'

'I was. Trust me. Sahara, this may be my last chance, but I really care about you.'

'Sorry, but I do not feel the same. I like you as a friend.'

'Why did you call me then?'

'Just to check on a friend and see how they were doing; is that a bad thing?'

'Perhaps not.'

There was a pause on both sides of the phone.

'Okay, nice to hear from you Sahara. I must go, there is someone waiting for me.'

'Who is the someone?'

'A friend, she was in my year level at Uni. We meet up for lunch now and again.'

At mention of the word 'she', Sahara's heart almost dropped into her stomach. What Sahara did not know was that there was nobody waiting.

'I must go Sahara. I'll call you later, now that I have your number.'

'If you must; bye.' Reluctantly Sahara hung up.

She checked her phone, waited and waited. There was no call for a week. A week became a month, and a month became six.

Following his return, Johnny was silent whenever his mother raised the topic of wife. Six months later, he desperately wanted to show his mother the photo of the young woman he had met but had to speak to her. He was worried and anxious about his mother's reaction. *What will mother think?*

Johnny finally pulled up the courage to show his mother two photos of the young woman. Her reaction blew him away. She narrowed her eyes and examined the two photographs closely with intent. She was in deep thought and murmuring to herself. Then she turned to Johnny, who all this while sat opposite her in absolute silence. He observed her facial movements as she scrutinised the photographs.

'Johnny, would you mind, allow me time to have a closer look at these … properly. Let's speak later, my son. I shall speak with you tonight.'

Johnny, not knowing what to do, left the room in silence. Ahbotta could be unpredictable. *Is she happy? Does she like her? Will she accept her?* Johnny spent the afternoon perturbed about Ahbotta's response to his choice of a prospective spouse.

That evening following dinner, mother called Johnny, as mothers would. As they settled into their chairs, she opened the *tête-à-tête*.

'My son, she has a nice face and beautiful eyes. I see she is tall. I have not seen her from the back, but her legs look strong. But son, she is only 'bones'. She is too small,' mother said slowly.

'Bones? What do you mean mother?'

'There is no *'meat'* on her!'

'She is beautiful.'

'Johnny, any woman you marry is also *my* wife. You children these days do not listen. Bones do not make children.'

'I know the culture, mother, but that does not make it right. Is that the only reason to marry?'

'Johnny, I am your mother! She has a nice face, she seems good, but she looks hungry, my child.' Using her left hand, and indicating with her thumb and index finger, Johnny's mother indicated how tiny the lady was. Shaking her head, she then sighed. 'With all the beautiful girls around, traditionally built, how could you only want this 'stick-thin' one? I want 'my wife' a little fuller, Johnny. Wide hips indicate fertility; it also means healthy children. The wife marries the family, not you alone Johnny,' his mother rebuked. 'What is her name? Is she from our people?'

'Her name is Sahara, and she is from our people mother. She lives in London. But I have not spoken to her for six months. I am not sure if she will accept. She called me but was not keen. I was at the time, but nothing really happened.'

'Do you have her number? I could call her and speak to her.'

Johnny felt he had nothing to lose. If mother wanted to know about her people, then she was at least interested. Mother was afraid Statina was the other option on the horizon. An option she could not accept.

The unpredictable mother; she did not like a skinny woman, now she wanted to call her. Is that to tell her off or…?

'I would like to know about her people and family.'

'If you must; here is the number.'

Then on the Sunday, exactly a week after that conversation between mother and son, Sahara's phone rang. It was a foreign number, which she recognised. She answered, but with hesitation.

'Hello Johnny! Oh, are you still alive?'

'This is not Johnny, it's his mother.'

'I'm sorry. I thought this was his number.'

'You are right. It is his number. Are you Sahara?'

'Yeeesssss,' she answered hesitantly.

'Johnny has not stopped talking about you.'

'Okay, I'm… I'm sorry,' she stammered.

'Don't be sorry, he loves you. Do you love him?'

'I, I… err… think of him sometimes.'

'Where are your parents?'

'It's a long story. I have my uncles and aunties.'

'We need to speak to them; if I want to have my son back. He is getting mad about you. Send me the contact numbers of your relatives.'

The call finished abruptly. Sahara was even more confused. *Now what did I do? I barely know this person?*

Johnny could not believe mother actually called Sahara.

'Mother, if you play with that girl, I will never marry another woman.'

'We need to know where she comes from, Johnny. We need her background. Get me those numbers I asked from her. There is *bad blood* in some families, and you know that.'

A few days later, after several phone calls, Sahara shared with Johnny the numbers of a relative and a close friend. Mother called them, and to her relief, they came from the same town. Turning to Johnny after one of the phone conversations, mother said:

'I did not know you were so intelligent! A girl who knows the way of my people! Now tell me, how does she look like?' 'Mother, have you not learnt enough to know that the rest will be fine? Keep the looks decision for me. You know more than enough. Let me decide one thing for myself in this process.'

'Is she like traditionally built? You know I do not like hungry looking women.'

'Mother, you are not me! The girl is for me, not for you. I showed you her photos before.' There was silence.

'Your wife is ours, not yours alone my son. Do not forget the ways of your people.'

The close scrutiny and background checks would last another twelve months. Mother finally approved of Sahara. Johnny was thrilled, but Sahara not so much. She wondered about the type of mother-in-law she was going to have following all that scrutiny. Johnny assured her on many occasions.

'You will like her. Mothers are all protective, as you will understand. She is caring and she is a good mother. She likes to know everything and is always in charge.

'That sounds like some of the mothers and aunties I know.'

'Then you shouldn't be surprised.'

Mother distrusted 'skinny' women. She thought they were hungry and troublesome. Worse were less fertile women. That's one of the reasons she disliked women like Statina, who had even told mother she was not keen on having children. To mother, that was the last straw. *God should deny one children. You do not deny yourself children.*

Mother often questioned herself about her own nurturing capabilities. Had she raised Johnny the way his grandmother would have desired? She constantly reminded Johnny of his role as the keeper of the family names. As for the females in the family and community, they were considered the keepers of culture and nationhood. There was the constant reminder of their distinct roles within a family.

Johnny is special, and his role to continue the next generation and keep his father's name alive was what his grandmother desired. As his mother, I must see to it he accomplishes that.

A 'suitable wife' was unarguable. Johnny never forgot how nervous he was as he sat and listened to mother speak to Sahara for the first time, and how she would later dissect Sahara's family and character during subsequent conversations. Today Sahara is part of Ahbotta and Johnny's people.

Thank God mother made that call.

It's been a decade since Johnny and Sahara first laid eyes on each other. Here they were now with two sets of twins. After the births of her twin boys and later twin daughters, Sahara was a 'respectable' size 16. She well met the requirement of her mother-in-law at this size.

Sahara had more flesh – assets for fulfilling traditional duties. *A sizeable African woman is the most desirable.*

'Sahara, my son is taking good care of you. Look at those hips! You are now a woman.'

'Ahbotta, I am fat, and I hate it!'

'Where do you come from? The pride of the man lies in his ability to fend for his family. The size of the wife is proof of that. Sahara, you are now a traditional woman. A bit more will be even better.

'I am size 16; do you really want me to be a size 18, Ahbotta?'

Size 18, my mother-in-law's ideal size for me, thought Sahara.

Sahara dreaded her size, not only because for health reasons, but also because of her wardrobe collection. Ahbotta desired more. Bigger for her was better. She fed her and the grandchildren.

'Sahara, have you eaten yet?'

'Yes, just had the *achu* and *fufu* corn with *achu soup* and vegetables.'

'Don't you want some yams?'

'No, I am so full!'

'But I prepared this for you! You are breast-feeding, you need to eat for you and the baby.'

'If I wasn't breast-feeding, you would say I am pregnant and need to eat for all three. When I was not pregnant, it was to look like a married woman. Always a reason to fatten me,' Sahara would grumble.

'I'll make you a cup of tea. Here is a piece of bread and some cake to have with it.'

'Use a small teacup please. No sugar, maybe one teaspoon.'

Sahara gave in, most times. There was no point trying to say no to Ahbotta. There was always the next thing, and then the next.

Ahbotta felt respected, and proud of her son and his wife. They gave her four grandchildren, something she thought might never happen. It was like a dream.

CHAPTER 11

Ahbotta

Ahbotta had prayed and hoped for the 'perfect' bride. Her ability to save money was only comparable to her capacity to 'scout' for a bride. Before Sahara, Johnny's mother kept a list of all the young maidens within their social circles that were two to five years younger than Johnny. Not only was she looking for the beauty from her beloved community; the right woman had to come from the right family.

Families would commence saving for bridal gifts once a girl child was born and betrothed. Such expensive gifts were meant to be a form of security to the young bride. Virgin brides were special, valued and respected. *Those were the ways of my people, Ahbotta's people.*

Johnny's mum professed that money should never be the criteria for a wife. Instead humility, character, and the family lineage and history were paramount.

Personal achievements were essential, but less important than these other qualities. Character was required, she had advised her children. Johnny's mother's other desire was 'to go home and honour the girl's family with the right *lobola or nkabehtooh* or *bride price* for raising their daughter well,' a symbolic gesture of gratitude to the in-laws and their community. For some nowadays, bride price has become a payment, and women have become a commodity. The concept has changed and been abused by greedy families, usually at the expense of the young couple.

Johnny resisted his mother's yearning for him to be married at eighteen. *Much too young,* Johnny thought to himself; but it was not, as far as mother was concerned. Ahbotta was twelve and Atonga was twenty-one years old when they 'married'. Her parents and in-laws had made this decision for them.

She was affianced at birth. Before her 'marriage' to *Atonga*, Ahbotta had never seen a naked male, let alone a penis on a man. She recalls the first night with Atonga. Following the marriage, Ahbotta moved to Atonga's compound and lived with Atonga's mother in her house. There was no contact between 'husband and wife' during that period of twelve months. She almost forgot she was married, as she was just another child in the house, until the day she saw stains on her under garments. She had been sitting down peeling coco-yams with Atonga's mother. As she stood up, she felt as if she had wet herself. It was unusual. On checking, she saw bloodstains. *I did not cut myself; if I did, it would be my hand'*. With a puzzled look on her face, she tried to hide what had happened, for fear of being scolded by Atonga's mother. But Atonga's mother had noticed what had happened.

'Go and wash yourself; I am coming.'

'I am finished, but the bleeding has stopped. I can't see the wound.'

'There is no wound, my child. You have just become a woman!'

Confused by such a statement, she struggled to process the words: *You have just become a woman.*

Atonga's mother provided her with some pieces of cloth to put between her legs every time she had blood. She had to sit on a special stool that week. She had to spend most of the day indoors. She felt ashamed and had to stay away from the other children. That week she was frightened, bewildered and became reclusive.

About a week later the family's women, including her biological mother, gathered at the Atonga compound. They chatted excitedly while the children ran around the compound. She was beginning to feel confident again now that the blood flow had stopped. Still no one explained to her what had happened to her body. *Has the wound inside of me healed?* she pondered.

One of the aunts took her into a room where other women were sitting and spoke to her lengthily. She nodded in affirmation all through the conversation, though she stared at her feet most of the time in reverence to the mothers and aunts. Atonga's mother, busy with preparations, joined them briefly to confirm what she had been told.

Ahbotta was a woman now and shall become a real wife.

It was not age that made her a woman; it was the blood flow, her first menstrual period.

That evening, Atonga's mother led her to the big house. *But that was where Atonga slept with the other older boys in the family. Atonga had a little room of his own. Why would I sleep in the boys' section of the compound? I have never entered there since I arrived here.* Ahbotta was very scared, but knew she could not refuse Atonga's mother command, who stood for her 'mother' in this compound. So Ahbotta did as she was told.

Until this week, she had been just another child in the household. Earlier in the day, she saw an aunt take new sheets into Atonga's room. Subtle gestures and hints were dropped to her at various points.

'You just have to be calm, and everything will be fine,' she was told by an elderly aunt.

Another directed her to wash herself that evening, which she did.

She was handed a new white nightdress. She was excited for her new clothes but scared at the same time. New clothes were a rarity, except during Christmas, for girls at her level.

The women chanted merrily all day. They clapped and danced. The songs were the same as when she was first brought to this compound twelve months ago. There was a lot of cooking, but she was told that the main celebrations would occur the next day.

At sunset, Ahbotta was escorted into Atonga's room. The party was led by Atonga's mother, followed by her mother, then by close female relatives, to the section of the house where Atonga slept. She was sat on a bed made up with white sheets. The bed looked attractive, but she did not want to leave a mess. She was frightened at the same time. So, she stood motionless and mute for five minutes.

The chanting continued, and so did the visitors. Then the women left the room, leaving her alone in there, where it was completely dark except for a small dim oil lamp burning in the corner. Her legs were quite sore by now, so she drew courage to sit on the edge of the bed. She was shocked at the images of naked women on the walls. Her parents and Atonga's mother would never have let her have pictures of naked men in her room. She would not want them anyway; *who would? Oh no, never! So, what were they doing there?*

She was almost dozing off, head bowed and held between her palms, when she heard footsteps followed by a voice, one that she recognised. It was Atonga's voice. *What is he doing here alone?*

He extended his hand towards her, but she pushed it away and jumped swiftly to her feet.

The room was not more than three meters square, poorly furnished by today's standards but tidy.

Atonga tried touching her hand first, but she moved away, frightened. What fate awaited her here?

After a few tries by Atonga, he turned to her and told her, 'You are my wife. That's why you're living here, and we waited for this day for a long time. Since you were born. It is our special night,' he whispered softly into in her ear. 'I will teach you everything.'

She had never sat so close to any male who was not her brother or father.

'Can I go to the toilet please?'

The toilet was outside, behind the house. She took the oil lamp with her. As she left the room, the corner of her eye caught Atonga undressing. *How could he undress with me in there? How rude!* she thought as she walked slowly to the latrine outside the house.

Instead of going to the toilet, she crept to Atonga's mother's window. She heard the voices of the women. They were speaking excitedly. Some close relatives had stayed over that night. Not her mother. She had her other relatives at home. They would join the others the next day at Atonga's compound, depending on the news.

Ahbotta scratched then knocked on Atonga's mother's window. There was sudden silence from within the hut. It seemed as if they expected the knock. Atonga's mother came out, accompanied by her sister. Calmly they walked her back to Atonga's room. She was in tears, but what could she do? She had nowhere to go, nowhere to run to, and no one would've received her if she did. Ahbotta knew what would happen if she returned. In fact, she had not paid a visit to her family for twelve months. If she ran away, she would be ostracised. As she had been reminded earlier in the day, she now 'belonged' to this family. So, she simply followed the two women, and she resigned her fate to Atonga and the elderly women.

She never detailed what happened but recalls the pain. It hurt a lot. The worst thing that happened that night was the blood – the stains on the sheets that morning, clear for all to see. Embarrassed and petrified, she feared the scolding that was likely to follow.

Came morning and everyone was celebrating, including the in-laws. Her parents were sent for, so they could see for themselves the evidence: the bloodstained bed sheets. This brought her mother extra joy and pride for raising her daughter well. It increased the bride price instantly. Festivities followed all day. For over a month friends and relatives brought food and palm wine to celebrate Ahbotta's marriage.

Ahbotta's mother began preparations for Ahbotta's homecoming immediately. This special homecoming occurred when Ahbotta was at term with her first pregnancy. Until such a time, she was forbidden to visit her family.

It would be years later that she understood the celebrations were about her virginity that she lost to Atonga. Was Atonga a virgin? Did it matter? Why did her virginity matter? That was such a long time ago.

Ahbotta received gifts, including a 24-carat gold necklace and earrings from her in-laws. Decades later, these same gifts became part of the gifts she would offer to her own daughter-in-law, Sahara.

'Back then the bride was respected, even though there could be a lot of pain. I know it was a long time ago. The world has changed, the people have changed and the cultures have changed.'

Johnny always listened attentively when Ahbotta spoke to him about her own marriage. 'Make sure your wife is a virgin when you marry, my son!' At that point Johnny smiled, stood up, kissed his mother on the cheek, then left the room. *Did Ahbotta expect a virgin girl to marry her son in 21st century Melbourne? She did try and did hope. Could Ahbotta say she was truly happy with what she went through?*

During her time, one did not use 'bad' words such as 'sex'. That continues today. Migration has not changed her. Many of these grandmothers, mothers, fathers and grandfathers still live in the world they left decades ago, a challenge for their children and grandchildren. Families may live together, but their minds can be worlds apart. The physical body may be here, but the mind is elsewhere.

Ahbotta had lost several pregnancies and infants. She recounts the three miscarriages and two stillbirths. Atonga abandoned her after the last stillbirth, blaming her for this misfortune. Ahbotta never remarried. She was scared of marriage but loved children. She decided to return home. To her surprise, her mother and father even welcomed her with open arms. 'If they had not, as a grown woman I knew what I would have done: leave.' The leave option was not activated; instead, her parents sympathised with their daughter. 'How my mother has changed!' If only Ahbotta had known that her father never wanted the marriage in the first place. He had had to succumb to pressure from the extended family and from cultural expectations.

'Johnny, you and your siblings are gifts from the almighty to me,' she often said. Though some of the other children had moved away, they were always in close contact with their mother. Two now lived in Australia; three lived with their husbands in China, and one in the UK. Ahbotta was not only fond of her children; she was proud of them.

Johnny was her only son; Ahbotta often referred to him as her 'miracle' gift. Johnny, her son, had to live with her till her last days as custom demanded. She had prayed for him to reach manhood all her life. She had kept all her life savings to buy gifts for Johnny and his wife and any children borne to them. She longed for that day, though she had little hope. But her experiences with Atonga and childbirth did not deter her – what did not break her heart gave her strength.

Johnny's wedding had been carefully planned from the day he passed his fifth birthday. It was meant to be unforgettable; it doubled as a celebration of his life. Today Ahbotta was a proud grandmother, and with Sahara, she could not have asked for more.

CHAPTER 12

Family and duty

Ahbotta adored Sahara, and the love was mutual. Sahara loved her new home in Melbourne. Poor Johnny could never 'hold his own between these two women'. You would never imagine that he brought them together, despite the mother scouting all those years for a perfect wife. He had 'found' Sahara, but Ahbotta had made that call. If anything, today Johnny looked more like the outsider. Both women loved Johnny as son and husband respectively. Their children loved him as father.

This intelligent ebony beauty was fashion conscious and quite stylish too. Sahara started to feel more comfortable shopping for her current size. As she walked past the last time, a dress caught her eye in one of the beautiful alleyways in Melbourne. It had the SALE tag on it too. She was drawn. She really liked the green dress with the pink embroidery around the neckline and yellow cross-stitch around the wrists. The length was just perfect, above her knees and now a handsome size sixteen. She thought this dress would do her womanly curves justice. Sahara was a size twelve prior to her marriage to Johnny – a size that her mother-in-law resented, until the children came along. She returned for the dress, but it was gone. She left disappointed.

Today was their family outing and shopping day, and Johnny took Sahara out to the mall. Sahara looked out for the same dress or similar ones in other shops. The twin boys were with them too. She found a lilac dress that she clearly saw herself in, imagining herself in the dress on a bright summer day in Melbourne. The linen fabric was light with rich bright colours. Embroidered rose petals in pink and red, they appeared so real. *The hands of an expert would have touched this piece.* Sahara thought it would fit perfectly and would match her mauve sandals, a gift from her mother-in- law.

At *Chique Boutique,* Sahara found the dress in her size and hurried into the fitting room to try it. Just as she finished undressing and was about to slip into the green dress, one of the older twins *Njinwi* crawled into the change room that she was in and flung the door wide open. It all happened so quickly. Worse, he leaned against the wide-open door and stretched his arms out for Sahara to pick him up. Sahara's clothes were on the hook behind the door, and the kid was leaning against the door, with the astonished eyes of an old fellow in the cubicle opposite hers. His mouth gaped; Sahara felt his eyes piercing through her, but she ignored the looks and directed her attention to Njinwi instead. She yelled at him, but the terrified boy simply froze in fright. Then he suddenly burst into laughter, thinking it was so funny. Sahara made a mental note that shopping malls would now be out of the question for a while.

Njinwi had been with his dad who was sitting on the 'man seat' patiently waiting for his wife, but he had slipped his father's gaze. *'This chapter will be closed until the boys and later the girls could put their hands over their head to reach the opposite ear.'* That was how decisions used to be made for whether children were old enough to understand their teachers when they first started school, Ahbotta had told her. It disadvantaged those with short stature as it took them longer to reach this milestone. Regardless, the decision was made.

Sahara dressed up hurriedly, then slammed the dressing room door behind her. She walked as fast she could, while holding her son's hand as firmly as she could. He screamed merrily, but her ears were deaf to his squeals.

As she left without the green dress, Sahara fumed with frustration, but what could she do?

She looked at the little boy but knew her hands were tied. *Yes, this child had rights. No smack, no cane, no screams – no nothing.* 'Ugh! Thank you, Australia!!' she sighed, as she shook her head vigorously. She wondered: *what would mother have done? I won't even go there! Just the look from the corner of her eye was enough to let me know what awaited me at home. The thought of me behaving half the way these kids do. Arrggh!* Sahara realised that her teeth were clenched, her head moving vigorously from side to side. *Who said it was fun having children? Did our mothers and grandmothers lie to us? Yes, there is something cute and special about these little ones, but not when they embarrass you publicly.* The two older boys could be mischievous; now the girls were taking after them too. They looked up to their brothers.

Johnny looked at the twins and smiled with joy. Johnny, Ahbotta and Sahara were on their way to the mall as they walked through the park. Johnny chatted happily about the twins. They inquired from Ahbotta what it was like carrying babies on their backs rather than pushing them in prams like this quadruple pram. Ahbotta was always too happy to share proudly the ways of her people; how such activities made their backs stronger and created strong bonds with their children. 'Today you use prams,' Ahbotta scoffed with displeasure.

Sahara recounted fondly the day she bought the quadruple pram, and how much easier it made her life. That was soon after the arrival of the second set of twins. The first set had not reached their fourth birthday at the time the other set entered the world, so they needed a pram that could carry all four. Sahara recalls the smiles and looks at the malls – usually positive, but occasionally that one evil eye. Those questioning eyes, as if Sahara was responsible for a 'genetic accident': egg cells dividing not once but twice after fertilization. Yes, her twins were natural twins, a normal occurrence, and relatively common among women from her part of the world. No IVF; just natural pregnancies. Ahbotta cherished the twins. She lived for them, she often said.

After many glances at shopping malls by shoppers, and tantrums from the boys, Sahara wondered why these shops all had to have their bright lolly jars, biscuits and other treats at children's eye level, and within their reach, when you queued at the checkouts. *What world that we live in? Marketing and profit making have taken over all aspects of life, even before the children were old enough to make any informed choices.* She had a love/hate relationship with malls, especially now with four young children in tow.

Ahbotta got the children ready for bed most nights. She thrived on it.

'It's bath time, kids; I can hear Ahbotta calling!' Sahara warned them.

It was *Bihnwi* and her sister *Chenwi*, and then the boys *Njinwi* and *Fonnwi*. The boys would call out to each other and do whatever they could to delay their bedtime.

'Can I have more dessert?' asked *Fonnwi*.

'You already had some more, and its bath time now. Boys, you have to go and have a bath now,' rebuked Sahara.

'I left my sandals behind. Can I go get them?'

'You two, stop stalling and go now to your grandmother!'

At that point, the boys knew that the line had been crossed and they had to make their way to the bathroom. They played this game most evenings to avoid going to bed on time. But they knew their mother's 'different' voice tones.

This was a 'smacking tone'; the voice for the last call before they received a little smack on the bum, and they both didn't like that. Two sets of twins inevitably meant busy times.

'I told you not to hide your sister's sandals!'

'I did not do it; he did it! It was *Njinwi*, not me!'

'It wasn't me alone! Your idea!' as he pointed to his brother.

'Now boys! Fonnwi, Njinwi, this is the last call! I need those sandals here NOW! I want you two in the bathroom in TWO MINUTES!' she screamed. 'What's wrong with you two?' Sahara gesticulated as she spoke.

'It's not me! It's your *good* grandson doing it!' *Fonnwi* complained to Ahbotta. 'You are the favourite one!' he turned to his brother.

'It's you!' pointing a finger at the other brother.

'It's YOU!!' repeating the gesture.

'Now, stop, and to the bath ... NOW!' Sahara said as she stepped in between the two brothers.

Sahara entered her ensuite, looking forward to a warm bath as she relaxed with one of her favourite books, 'Things Fall Apart'. *Finally, the day is over, I can now sit back and reflect on the day's events and plan for the next day.*

As she read 'Things Fall Apart', by the Nobel prize- winning Nigerian writer Chinua Achebe, for the ninth time, she felt inspired. This man's work has inspired many writers globally, with a huge impact on African writers who write their own stories about their own people. He even wrote about depression: he mentioned the word when the ill-fated Ikemefuna remembered his mother and little sister while at Okonkwo's household. As Sahara read the chapter about Ikemefuna, she thought, *would women have made the same decision if they had been the clan's leaders? Thankfully Nwoye's mother, Okonkwo's first wife, treated*

Ikemefuna like her son; she nurtured and supported him, but she could not protect his life. She was only a woman and couldn't interfere in the decisions of the men, the decision-makers of the clan. That was back in 1958 when this book was written. Some six decades later, people still talk about the lack of recognition of mental illness in African cultures, and too many women still feel like Nwoye's mother.

Sahara turned and admired her glowing blemish-free silky-smooth skin in the bath. Sahara detested skin bleaches. She was an advocate for natural beauty, and a conversation she had had years earlier had helped her to embrace her natural beauty. *The hydroquinone and chemicals in bleaches aged one so quickly that a woman in her twenties could easily look decades older. Some bleaching agents simply turn dark skin into 'red skin',* she thought. Sahara detested these chemicals. *Have a look at the knuckles of women and girls who bleach. You wouldn't want to eat the food they serve.*

Sahara once heard about a teenager who detested her own mother's food because of bleaching. 'Her hands looked horrid, with blotches everywhere,' the young woman had told Sahara.

Sahara recalled a conversation with an older woman she met, with pink, blue, black and red skin, all in one body. Sahara in her true spirit, and as politely as she possibly could, asked about her bleaching with hydroquinone, and its risks.

The response: 'Fairer skin is more beautiful, and people with fairer skin have more respect in society, earn more money and have more opportunities, compared to us with darker skin tones.'

'Really, Aunty?'

'True.'

'Is that why you bleach: for opportunity and acceptance?'

'You do not understand! Try looking for a job! You will be lucky if you ever reached the interview stage; even luckier if they actually offer you the job! Stop and think about upward mobility. That's another story for another day! You do not understand now, but you will have to, one day.'

'I hear you; but do you understand the risks to you?'

'Remember you also have to deal with the name aspect.'

That was her response.

Sahara had listened attentively to the Aunty as they drank *Shatiki* coffee in the beautifully decorated room. The more she heard, the more she became emotional; and the more heard, the more she learnt about the people she thought she knew and was a part of. Tears flowed from her eyes. She could not understand why she was crying, but the emotions were certainly there. This Aunty had just lifted a burden from her chest that she may have carried for a long time. More was to come, and it was too much for Sahara. The two women hugged each other, as they both wept.

As they spoke, another young woman had joined them. She sat quietly and listened without uttering a word. She introduced herself as Amina. She had moved interstate thrice and from one town to another five times, trying to find suitable and meaningful work. Amina wanted to work; she loved work. This was some years ago, but the memory was still so fresh for Sahara.

Just as she slipped into her nightdress, Johnny walked into the room and smiled at her. She was half naked.

Before the children were born, Sahara and Johnny had weekly date nights, and every week was different. Their conversation went something like this:

'Eh Sahara, it's Friday night, what do you have planned?'

'Oh Johnny, a stroll along the beach at sunset will be nice!'

'That sounds like a good idea.'

'We can then have dinner at any of the nearby restaurants.'

'Count me in!'

'You are in.'

Now those spontaneous dates were gone. The children had to be factored into every decision. While Ahbotta was handy and helped out, they were reluctant to burden her with the children. They had to be sure that Ahbotta was doing it because she loved and enjoyed it, not because she felt she had to.

The red gown that Sahara slipped into tonight was a gift from Johnny. It was an oversize Valentine's Day gift; they had made love that night with passion. It was only the two of them back then, though Ahbotta was around. The aroma from Johnny's scent had filled the room when he walked in. The fragrance from the French perfume had rich aromas from an ancient concoction – *Chique Cosmetiques* do not share their recipes. The smell was masculine. Johnny took deep hard breaths as he made love to Sahara. It was full of passion.

Johnny had entered her and thrusted hard. The movements became more rapid. His hands were all over her body. Johnny cried out as he took deep hard breaths. They both climaxed, then Johnny had rolled over and fallen asleep almost immediately. It was their first Valentine's Day together as a married couple. It was special; she loved it. He loved her.

Sahara loved the sleekness of this gown. She loved the sensation of the delicate soft silk, so redolent of the memories and secrets that came with it. Johnny smiled every time she wore this lingerie. It was one of the few times they could communicate without needing words.

Tonight, had been similar to the night she first laid eyes on this gown. It slips on well, though perhaps not quite as perfectly as it once fitted. When first bought, it was free and quite loose; the silk was soft and the fabric delicate. The finishing had silk lace overlays. She never asked Johnny the cost but thought it must have been expensive. After another passionate night, they were both tired and fell asleep in each other's arms.

Johnny was not a morning person, and after a 'busy night', she simply left him alone. Sahara went downstairs to make herself a coffee. As she was about to take the first sip, the doorbell rang. It was a courier holding a parcel from *Chique Boutique*. As Sahara signed for the parcel, she heard a call from one of the four: *Maaammmaaa!*

Sahara knew that her quiet time in the morning was now over. She had only the first sip of her coffee. Once one of the children was awake, within a few minutes the others would be up too. *Do they all have some internal communication device that I do not know of?* Sahara wondered. The girls would usually wake up first, and then call out; within minutes their brothers would be awake. The girls had learned to climb out of their cots now – if they couldn't, one of the older boys was keen to lend them a hand. Ahbotta was in the room next door, always willing to help with these four.

Though Ahbotta had a granny flat, she would spend up to three nights every week with Sahara, Johnny and the children in the main house. She did it when the boys were born. When Sahara and Johnny found out that there was another set of twins on the way, she convinced the family to buy a larger family home. Ahbotta planned to move in permanently this time. She had made a secret offer on a huge house, two streets away from their current home, before expressing her wishes to the family. Ahbotta always did what she thought was needed to assist Johnny and Sahara. It took a lot of negotiation, as Sahara did not want to move. She was worried about costs. *Had it all been planned?* Sahara wondered where they would get the money.

'My daughter, I am an old woman. When the war broke out I ran, but not empty-handed.'

'I know you took the children; Johnny is the evidence.'

'That's not what I mean, Sahara. I had gold and I had it with me all the time.'

'How did the soldiers and others not take it?'

Smiling, Ahbotta responded: 'I had it where they could not go near. I only took it out whenever I sat down to urinate.'

'Enough, I have heard enough!'

'No, you have not! You, young people like to know things; come sit down, here,' pointing to the chair Sahara had sat on.

Sahara had heard enough and wasn't ready for any further details just yet.

CHAPTER 13

Inclusion

Now expecting another set of twins, Sahara planned to stop work two months before her due date. But by the fifth month of her pregnancy, she felt exhausted, and needed early release from work. Sahara was quite large compared to the boys' pregnancy, and her feet and hands were swollen. She had developed pre-eclampsia and gestational diabetes. The plan was to stay in hospital and get the support she needed, with meals carefully planned and sugar levels monitored. She was otherwise well enough, but with twins, was it best for her to stay in hospital? Sahara's obstetrician, Dr Awek Dang, an Australian of South Sudanese ancestry, suggested it. Ahbotta was a skilful negotiator; she had even promised 'on her mother's grave' that she would do everything for Sahara at home. She was supported by her midwife *Emechi*, born in Nigeria, and by Dr Osbourne, from the UK.

Ahbotta could no longer keep the secret of her wealth – a lot of wealth – and her *profession* too. Her grandmother had been a traditional birth attendant, a skill that was later handed down to her own mother, *Na Shettu*. Between them, these two women helped hundreds of women to give birth safely. Her grandmother 'trained' many women, some who later went to school to become trained health professionals. Their family had a respectable reputation for safe home deliveries.

Like her mother and grandmother, Ahbotta had planned to become a traditional birth attendant. But her mother had other plans for her: for an education and a life she hoped would be much better than hers. Ahbotta went to the newly created Teachers Training College in her town, where she trained for three years and graduated as a primary school teacher. Her studies were in her local language.

As a child, Ahbotta assisted her mother and grandmother to support pregnant women. When the new government requested traditional birth attendants to register births and send records to the central registry, it was Ahbotta who filled the forms on behalf of her mother and grandmother. She also had the living experience of giving birth herself. Her own experiences made her wise, and she was determined to see her grandchildren arrive in this world healthy and safe.

She understood why Sahara had to be on strict bed rest until term. But it was difficult to convince the midwife and the doctors that she preferred her daughter-in-law to be at home, and that she was able to support her at home. The healthcare team decided to convene a meeting where the decision was made for Sahara to stay in hospital.

There was another family in a similar situation, the Smith family. Mercy Smith was expecting triplets, in her third pregnancy. Like Sahara, Mercy suffered from pre-eclampsia. She too was advised to have strict bed rest in hospital, but she and her husband simply refused. She cited the care of the other two children as a reason that she was unable to stay in hospital. Her husband James, the breadwinner of the family, worked in the transport industry. He was unable to care for the children and earn if Mercy was kept in hospital. The stakes were certainly high for this young family, but the risks to Mercy's health and that of the unborn babies were even higher. After prolonged discussions with Mercy, it was agreed that Mercy could go home to South Melbourne. The midwives believed that Mercy was careful and could be trusted with her health decisions. 'Mercy also understands every word of English,' one of the midwives remarked.

Mercy was known to be a heavy smoker who drank socially with friends. Though she did not stop with the pregnancies, she was still allowed to go home. When asked why she would not stop, Mercy always referred to the other two children: 'I didn't stop with them, and they're normal, so why should I stop with these?'

Both children were not physically disabled but suffered from ADHD. Thomas Jr. was uncontrollable without his medication. Following Thomas's diagnosis, he was put on strict medication and diet. Mercy often forgot to give Thomas his medication. The husband, Thomas Sr, was often away at work and would return home to a house with toys everywhere. A loving husband, Thomas would quietly plead with Mercy what to do with the two older boys.

Mercy's home was a modest three-bedroom brick veneer house with a tiled roof, in one of the best streets in their suburb. You could easily refer to it as, 'the worst house on the best street'. Thomas Sr had inherited it from his adopted parents. He was their only child, and they had showered him with love. He was not good with school but could not be faulted with his manners. He met Mercy in Year 10 at the local high school. They were childhood sweethearts. They married in a lavish but private ceremony at the local Catholic Church in their early-twenties. They began their family soon after, and the children arrived in quick succession. Thomas was soft spoken and gentle. Mercy was plain but sometimes feisty.

Her mother and grandparents together had raised Mercy and her three brothers. Theirs was a house of chaos. Her mother tried to be strict, but every attempt to discipline her four children made the next attempt more difficult, as the kids simply ignored her soft voice. She would generally succumb to the pressure. Mercy's father passed away when the second of four siblings was only five years old. Her youngest brother was a year old then. Mercy's mother worked hard to raise the children. It was difficult. With limited resources, Mercy and her siblings were given the best their mother could.

While Mercy and her siblings could be unruly with each other, they loved each other too. They were close and remained so. Two of the boys went on to graduate from university and the other became a successful mechanic who owned a garage with six employees. Mercy, 'the family princess' as they would refer to her, depended a lot on her mum for support. Mercy had received and enjoyed her company and support, until that fateful day when her mother suffered a massive heart attack. She was rushed to the Hospital where she passed away after a week in intensive care. Mercy's family had to make the decision to turn off her ventilator. Had she lived, they were advised that she was going to be a 'vegetable'. For a woman who had been so independent, her children followed her wish not to be held back should she be in a vegetative state requiring permanent care. The children found it hard to accept but respected her wish. It was a turning point for Mercy and her family.

Mercy was inconsolable and turned to alcohol. She was a smoker prior to this sad event, but following her mother's demise, Mercy became a chain smoker. Thomas Sr. found it hard to bear but stood by Mercy. She had bared her history to the hospital. They had sympathy for Mercy and thought she would be 'fine' at home. She could read instructions, and she could understand every word they said.

Ahbotta had little English but was definitely knowledgeable. Arabic, Swahili and *Ngemba* were her *lingua franca*. She understood there was a handicap in communication, and always requested an interpreter. On this occasion, a male interpreter was sent to assist the family.

The interpreter – Solomon, or *Solo* as he was called – had arrived in Australia as an accompanied spouse under the class 457 visa category. Prior to migration he had trained as an engineer, but later found it hard to get his qualifications recognised in Australia. His family had mortgaged their land to get him through university in his home country. Solo's mother *Ma Sineh* was the strictest woman possible, respected for her fairness and honesty. She mothered her nieces and nephews. She would step in to support *Solo* whenever she could. That was the only way they could move ahead, she would stress.

With the support of family, Solo successfully graduated in Engineering from the prestigious Akerela University, one of Africa's oldest and most highly regarded Universities. He graduated with honours, but since his arrival a decade ago, had struggled to find work in his field. He was advised to do a Certificate III course in Aged Care Services. 'This is a sure pathway to income,' his friends advised. 'Forget about all those degrees.' Solo refused to listen to this advice. Instead he commenced and completed a Master's Degree in Engineering (MSc.E) within two years from another prestigious university in Melbourne. But Solo still could not secure ongoing employment in his field of expertise and training. He took on temporary roles, but none progressed him towards ongoing employment. Solo began to wonder if it was a myth that there was a shortage of engineers.

Solo's wife recently bumped into her high school maths teacher, Mr Adiya. He taught her when she was fourteen years old. There was hardly a maths problem he could not solve. Adiya, like Solo was a young graduate at the time he taught her. Adiya was so good at maths. Adiya began teaching students not too far off his own age in the local high school. Solo's wife still referred to him as 'Mr Adiya.' The students loved Adiya, not only for the contents of his brains and good looks but also for his good sense of humour and easy-going nature. He could show off his mathematical skills in ways that were unimaginable. The kids loved that too; they would show up to class even if they did not understand the 'integration equation' or how to 'find X'. They would later complete high school with knowledge of 'demand and supply' integration and factorisation. That could be attributed to the genius of Adiya.

Adiya could solve any maths problem and make it seem as simple as a, b, c. Even as an adult today, Solo's wife was still in awe of Adiya's mathematical genius. She was therefore stunned that he had not been able to secure an interview in any institution to teach maths, following his arrival in Australia some three years ago. He had even moved interstate twice to search for work in his field but he did not have the local experience they required. Solo's wife wondered, *how would Adiya or Solo ever have local experience if no one ever opened the local doors?*

With his ability to speak five languages, Solo turned to interpreting. His passion was mathematical engineering, but he needed his sanity and dignity. He was a man with 'balls' and was raised to believe that a real man worked hard and provided for his family. Not only had he migrated under a woman's visa, he was almost dependent on her for survival, he would tell his friends. He was beginning to slip into depression.

At the time of his departure there were three female elected members of parliament. Today there are thirty such women in his country's parliament. Solo was still living in the country he remembered growing up in, where the men led and the women followed. It could be likened to living with Okonkwo in 'Things Fall Apart' as a wife.

When Solo arrived at the hospital and was introduced to Ahbotta and Sahara, Solo asked for Sahara's husband immediately. Sahara turned and stared at Ahbotta. They looked at each other somewhat hesitantly. Solo proceeded.

'You must be Sahara and you, the mother?'

'I am her mother-in-law.'

'I am Solomon, call me Solo, I am the interpreter.'

'Nice to meet you, Solo, I am Sahara. Glad you are here.'

'Where's your husband?'

'He must be out somewhere in the courtyard. He may come in during our conversation.'

'I will like him to be here. He is the head of the family, so I think I will need him.'

'You are right, he is a man, but I am the one to push out the babies,' Sahara responded sarcastically, before turning to Ahbotta. 'Can you get the head of the family? I mean Johnny.'

The two women looked at each other, while Solo had his head slightly bowed.

'Err; you do not want Johnny here? He is your husband.'

'I know he is, but I'm sure I can make this decision and his mother is here. She will be fine.'

A midwife and a doctor joined them shortly after, they interrupted the discussion.

'The interpreter is here now Sahara to help your mother- in-law. Hello, Mr Solomon. Good to see you again.'

'Hello Doctor Osbourne, and Nurse…?'

The discussion between Sahara, and the healthcare team went smoothly. Johnny came in almost at the end.

Solo did his job diligently, but his demand to have the husband in the room disturbed Sahara.

Sahara had mixed feelings, as she understood the cultural impositions on Johnny and from her extended family back home in their country should anything go wrong. But for a woman who considered herself modern, she wondered about the interpreter's behaviours. *How could culture that was made by people hold them back from moving forward?* she questioned.

Staying in bed for the next few months was a challenge for Sahara, but she knew and understood why it had to happen. It took a month of convincing her midwives and doctors that she would be perfectly fine at home. She had all the help and support one could ask for. Sahara wondered why it took them so long, to allow her to take her bed rest at home. 'Was it not evident that Ahbotta was very capable of helping her at home?' She wondered about Mercy and how she was coping.

Sahara approached a midwife assigned to her during her third week of stay in the hospital. Johnny was always on standby. She wondered why the delay.

What she did not realise was that during handover, she had been handed over to the staff as 'demanding and difficult'. This placed a barrier between her genuine requests and trying to be understood by the next team and the next one after that. The message got handed over from one team to the next without anyone questioning the basis for it.

It was Sr. Catherina, a midwife who had worked in Uganda for three decades who finally questioned the rationale for not engaging Sahara in the decision. She had the cultural knowledge and understood the nuances. It did not take long before Sahara was free to go home where she would spend the rest of her three months at home and only return for routine observations. Thank God for the call from Afrika, who had crossed paths with Sr. Catherina during one of her many relocations. 'A friend's friend is a friend.' It meant Sr Catherina could call on Afrika, just in case. *Networks are necessities in life.*

At home, Sahara struggled to let Ahbotta allow her walk to the bathroom instead of using a wheelchair.

'Sahara, here is the pan for you, or I bring the wheelchair to take you in there, if it's number two.'

'Ahbotta, I have only one thing to ask you every day.

Can I go to the bathroom by myself? Just this one time?' 'No, Sahara.'

'Just want my feet to feel the ground. Stretch my muscles.'

'I will call the lady to come massage your feet, or your husband should do it, eh?' With a smile Ahbotta turned to Sahara and using her index finger to point at Sahara 'I made a promise to the sisters and the doctors Sahara.'

'Ahbotta, just for once, can you let me walk?'

'No. What would you like to eat?'

Sahara felt like a child again. She sighed and at this point, realised it was pointless trying to negotiate with her 'strict' mother-in-law. However, Sahara appreciated Ahbotta's role that ensured this 'home stay' did not swerve.

Today with happy cuddles, healthy twins she appreciates everything about Ahbotta, even when she is bossy.

Mercy lost the triplets tragically. She almost lost her own life if not for the diligent healthcare professionals who acted swiftly when she was brought in by ambulance. It was too late for the little ones.

CHAPTER 14

Mumene and Afrika

Mumene and Afrika, unlike their fellow students had lived like princesses. They had money and security. Their lives were nothing like those of their fellow students. They could afford the designer clothes, the designer shoes, and the designer handbags. They had it all. They lived in the best apartments in town and went for weekends in the coastal resorts of Davidson and Liberty. Weekends were often spent on the sparkling beaches swimming and basking in the sun. After all they had money. *How did they earn money*, poor students often wondered? Sofia was one of those students and her mother was, Mamie Murphy. She gave Sofia just enough to get by. Sofia was now friendly with Mumene. Mumene and her friends had excess. Mumene was generous with her friend and had no problem 'helping' friends out. Their mothers visited them on campus bimonthly. Occasionally, Mamie

Murphy would ask to join Madam and her driver when she came visiting her daughter. It would not have been affordable otherwise.

Afrika considered her mother well to do; they lived in one of the 'normal' neighbourhoods of the capital city. What is wealth; love or money? She had an abundance of the former.

Now, like children from the most affluent backgrounds, Mumene had to study at the same university, Achieve W. University. Afrika had done extremely well with the entrance exams to university, scoring 'A' grades in all her four units. With 'A' grades in Maths and Economics, Afrika's future path in Accounting was cemented. With no credits, her payments and all expenses had to be paid upfront. Rents had to be paid up front for twelve months, in addition to purchasing textbooks and fees. Her mother's *Akirteh* group was a 'savings bank'. The women came together monthly and contributed. The money was handed to one member. A different member collected the money at every sitting until everyone had had her turn. This process went around until all members of the group had received their rightful share of the contributions. Often there was no interest but if any, it was minimal. What was earned as interest, during the course of the year was later redistributed to group members in cash or in kind. With often no bank accounts to their names, these women were savvy, and not a penny went missing. These *Akirteh* groups were built on trust within the community.

Like most of her fellow students, Mumene did not make the decision to study what she enrolled in. Her teachers made the decision for her and for most of the others, in areas the students excelled in rather than on what they liked. Coincidentally Afrika loved numbers, but that was not the case for many others. Mumene got into fashion studies in the beauty department. This course required average students. Though Mumene had done well enough to get into other departments. Honourable used his influence so she could study what she wanted: Fashion.

Sofia and Mumene grew up in the same neighbourhood, but their worlds could not be more different. Mumene was a year older than Afrika and two years older than Veronique. Mumene's father was a roving businessman nicknamed Honourable. Honourable had companies across the continent.

He called his wife Madam, his 'director of home affairs' who was actually a former teacher. She managed him too, though often at a cost. No one remembers the source of the name Honourable, however the locals honoured him and his money. He was generous with it, that could not be denied.

Sofia was the eldest of four children. Mumene her friend had been brought up in wealth. Mumene grew up in a beautiful mansion in the exclusive suburb of *Astobas*, in the capital city.

Every house in this neighbourhood was fenced and gated. The gatemen were ever ready to open and close the gates whenever someone arrived. The drivers opened the car doors for her, and if her friends were present, the same applied to them. She went to private schools and colleges all her life and was now studying at the prestigious *Achieve W. University*. The period at the local, though Prestigious Achieve W University, also served as a waiting period for Mumene. She was waiting for admission to either Cambridge or the Australian International University. If successful, Mumene would travel to the UK or Australia. Her parents could afford the tuition. Mumene had been to Europe and America for holidays before but not to Australia. While she enjoyed the shopping and the other luxuries in London and New York, her only concerns were that they did not have the staff and maids she was used to back home.

Whenever her family visited England, Madam had to cook their own meals.

'Who is preparing dinner for us this evening?' Asked Honourable.

'Mother?'

'I am exhausted from the day at the mall. Dragging all those shopping bags.' Madam replied.

'But we have to eat,' thundered Honourable's voice.

'Ma Terrie is not here. Mummy, would you cook?'

'You two did not hear me, right? We could go to that place we ate at last night.'

'But the food was… not tasty,' Mumene said.

'Family, I am tired. Can you and your father do the cooking?' said Madam.

'When did I become your servant?' Honourable rumbled. 'I earn the money in this family! You are here because of my hard work and I need to cook?

When did men start cooking for their wives in my house? Did you marry me or did I marry you? I paid the dowry, all of it. I even went to people that I was not supposed to. Now you tell me you are tired and I should cook?'

'Daddy, mummy works hard just like you? We never ever see you. She is here most of the time. We have servants and others to help her back home, but dad, mum works damn hard. Dads can also cook you know? I can help you.'

On that note, Mumene moved closer to her dad, and leaned on his shoulder; which was just as well.

Honourable was just about to get up and pounce on Madam.

Madam walked away and did not come out of her room until the next day.

Mumene and her dad got some fast food for dinner.

Madam complained how difficult it was to adjust to life without servants. But she and the children covertly enjoyed these periods away, and not only because of the beautiful scenery; it was the one time they could be together as a normal family.

Mumene often fantasised seeing her father doing parental duties like shopping for groceries, cooking, cleaning, watching over his own children and occasionally even playing with them.

Back home Mumene hardly saw their father; Ma Terrie and nannies raised the children. Madam was there but had to deal with the big receptions and play the role of wife with the countless visitors and groups Honourable had. Ma Terrie became the default mother to the children and her own daughter Afrika, another 'sibling' friend of the family.

Madam would consult Ma Terrie on almost everything about the children. When the puberty blues hit, it was Ma Terrie who knew what to do. Aside from these children, she had raised her own children, the youngest being Afrika. Afrika became close friends with Honourable and Madam's children especially the two closest to her in age. Afrika became aware of another world through her mother's work. Ma Terrie was not *affluential* but vowed her children would never live her life.

As Mumene grew older, she thought of the places she had visited. As children, play between these rich children and Ma Terrie's children was initially restricted, though Ma Terrie fostered and nurtured the bond between the children from an early age. Madam loved Ma Terrie, despite the occasional squabbles between the two women. Some of these squabbles were because Ma Terrie, would bring her children to work.

'Madam, if Afrika cannot come with me or play with the other children while I work, I shall leave. They are in the same age group.'

'Ma Terrie, you should be at work, not caring for your child.'

'Well, this work is in your house, not at an office. I know this is your office.' Ma Terrie added mockingly. 'Afrika, climb on my back. Let's go home.' She added as she lowered herself to a squatting position for Afrika to climb.

Madam expected fifty guests that night. Ma Terrie, the head maid, had just walked out. And one of the maids had been off ill for the day; she was expecting a baby.

Within an hour there was a knock at Ma Terrie's door. It was Madam's driver.

'Ma Terrie, Madam sent me to come fetch you. Are you ready?'

'Musa, just leave me alone, tell her to do the cooking and the cleaning. If Afrika cannot come with me, then I can't either. She is one of the children. You heard me. She is one of them.'

On that statement, Musa's mouth was ajar but he did not think much about it, and never said a word. He focused on the mission: to get Ma Terrie return to work.

Musa delivered the message from Ma Terrie to Madam as intended.

Madam accompanied Musa this time to Ma Terrie's house, twice within an hour. When they arrived, Musa stayed in the car. Madam hopped out of the car and called for Ma Terrie.

Afrika was playing outside with her siblings; she recognised Madam and ran towards her. Madam, though hesitant, picked Afrika up. It was the first time she did this. This was similar with her own children; hugs were reserved for Ma Terrie and the maids. Madam for the first time noticed that there was ample resemblance between Afrika and Mumene. She shrugged her shoulders, *they are all children, they look and behave the same,* she thought. After much convincing, Madam and Ma Terrie together with Afrika returned to prepare and welcome the evening's guests.

Did Honourable have anything to do with Afrika's paternity? No, no, it can't be; she is only a maid. That rumour, but how?

Madam suppressed such thoughts immediately. They were evil.

Honourable encouraged Madam to allow some more liberty to Ma Terrie after he heard of the previous day's events. Ma Terrie was more than a maid to her. They had built a deep trust over the years. She could carry Afrika, on her back occasionally while doing her chores. The bond between mother and daughter was strong, and that applied to the other children. Money could be scarce, but love was abundant. Mumene would refuse to eat if Ma Terrie turned up without Afrika on weekends. Afrika became one of the fixtures within this family. Honourable was 'fond' of Afrika too, which sometimes made Madam resent her.

As Afrika grew up, the exposures to both of her two worlds caused her and Mumene to become socially conscious. Though Afrika never had the opportunity to travel abroad with Mumene's family and their network of friends, she realised there was another humanity out there. A world she craved for and a life she desired for her mother and her own unborn children. Her outlook on life had been unconsciously but surely changed.

Upon their first return from abroad when she was six, Mumene shared stories about the beautiful streets of London and the clean City Hall. Her conversations did not end with her friends; she occasionally asked her parents questions in front of guests. Honourable was sometimes baffled or outright embarrassed by Mumene's questions.

Today dinner was with the French, English, German and Swiss Ambassadors. Some influential businesswomen and men were also present. Honourable and his wife were hosting them at their residence situated below the iconic slopes of Mount Louis.

Mumene ran in uninvited to speak to her father as they conversed about the roads of Astobas.

'Why could they not build the roads in Astobas and around the country like those of London? We have a lot of money daddy, and your friends too!' Mumene said.

'Well, it's the job of the government to build roads and infrastructure, Mumene.'

'Who is the government daddy?'

'The Minister and all the people with the President.' He replied.

'But you have many friends that you said work with the President and are rich and are Ministers, daddy.' She interrupted again. 'Ask them to help the poor people.'

Such questions were not uncommon from Mumene. It was an innocent question from an innocent child. Her father was not only puzzled by her daughter's questions but felt embarrassed as he knew his country had the money to build roads, markets, libraries; the wealth was not only unevenly distributed, but was in the hands of only a few people. And he was one of them. He thought to himself, what does an eight-year-old know about development, and libraries, and life?

Mumene sometimes questioned, why the drivers were there with them all the time.

Why did drivers have to pick them up from school rather than the parents? Why did her parents not collect her from school, even once?

Why did the cook have to serve the meals to her mum and her dad and her siblings? Why wouldn't they sit together with them at the table?

She had wondered about their neighbour, Mamie Murphy, an imposing woman in her late-forties. *Why did her house look like it did?*

Only this time the audience was not only her family. The friends and decision makers were sitting right there. They heard her. Honourable asked for Madam to take the child away to her nanny.

'Sometimes Mumene, you speak like someone asked you to,' Honourable told Mumene. There was silence in this truth. They must have been reflecting about what this eight- year old girl had said. There was uneasiness in the room.

The Swiss Ambassador instead had his eyes fixated on the surrounding mountains. The views at this time of the day, just as the sun was setting and piercing through the mountains, were extraordinary. Depending on which balcony you were on or where you sat at the reception area of this mansion, one could see the whole city, its hills and undulating chain of mountains.

Located on a plateau, *Astobas* was a beautiful place. It was surrounded by a chain of mountains created millions of years ago as a result of volcanic activity. The soil was dark and rich, the scenery, vivid green. From where he sat, the Swiss Ambassador could see the waterfalls from the Mibi River. The ten-meter waterfall was separated into two by a large rock in the middle, lending it the name, 'the fertility fall' by the locals.

Women who struggled to fall pregnant went and bathed in the Mibi pool, at the bottom of the waterfall; those that desired twins did it twice. The pool was also separated by another large rock into two smaller pools; this affirmed Mibi's place in the minds of the locals as the fertility place. One of the pools was calm, unlike the other that received the main flow from the fall. Local children would swim in the calm pool but never in the other. Surrounding the fall were green shrubs and ancient vegetation. The flowers regenerated themselves every year. The sea of Water lilies and Canna lilies marvelled every visitor. From where the Swiss Ambassador sat, he delighted on the perfection of this creation. *What aptness,* he day dreamed.

A successful businessman, commanding five transport agencies, two coffee and cocoa plantations and dozens of tea plantations in the country, and across the continent, Honourable had influence. He also raised funds for his friends who ran for political office.

Honourable had been married three times and had twenty official children to six women. Some were his concubines. Madam was his third wife, a local beauty from his hometown. They had met through an acquaintance after the end of his second marriage. It had been at another occasion not dissimilar to this; Madam was there helping out and had served Honourable. Now she is the dame of the house.

During such occasions, Honourable would invite his neighbours, as culture dictates. Some of the local elders would also receive invitations to receptions at the residence. These elders were his eyes and ears locally, and occasionally he 'oiled their lips' too. He gave them 'little sums', which to them were large sums as they could work for six months or more to earn such money.

The fine china and crystals had been polished earlier in the day. This evening, everything was laid out perfectly for the evening's guests. Madam and the maids spent days, sometimes weeks, ensuring that everything was going to be perfect. Madam's friends were always on the guests list. These women, who used to be in obscurity until Madam married Honourable, were now part of the society. Worthy of note, were two of Madam's friends, Betsie and Bella; she had grown up with. They were all beauties. Madam had won the local beauty pageant, but all three (Madam, Betsie and Bella) had participated. This victory had cemented her position within this group of friends: the beauty among the beauties.

Like her, Bella and Betsie had managed to get themselves through university. They got into public service and had little recognition until their friend married Honourable. With Madam's help, Bella and Betsie secured positions within Honourable's company as directors. This meant frequent travels and frequent shopping. Betsie shopped designer shoes and handbags, and Bella clothes and jewellery. Madam liked everything: shoes, bags and clothing. Bella and Betsie also doubled as Madam's private detectives on Honourable, who had a wondering eye for women.

Madam had a hairdresser who visited her home twice weekly to ensure her hair was impeccable; her name was Marie-Noelle. Marie-Noelle knew the local gossip and fed madam with stories she would otherwise have little or no access. Marie-Noelle became a third friend.

What Madam and her three friends, could likely wear to parties was always one of the speculative topics of conversations for guests. These women planned outfits for weeks and maybe months ahead. There was always gossip in the community, about whether Betsie and Bella had other responsibilities apart from looking after themselves. Bella had a son and Betsie twin daughters but both women were single, by choice.

Betsie's mother would scorn her for not settling down. Betsie's mother loved Madam for the decision to be married. Betsie was always frank with her mother; 'Yaya, why bother, when you have everything and can do what you like. Freedom, freedom Yaya!' Bella had retorted when her mother disapproved of her being single at thirty-five. Bella and Betsie's children also lived with their mothers. They provided their mothers with the financial support required for the children's needs, as their mothers raised their children on their behalf.

Mumene recalls the housemaid mostly in their cleaning clothes. Ma Terrie changed on arrival every morning into her maid's uniform and at the end of the day changed back into her denims. The two women, Madam and Ma Terrie, were of similar build and size. Mumene's mum passed on her 'old' clothing to her friends, occasionally to the extended family, and from time-to-time, she would reward the maid with an outfit for some new initiative or for doing something outstanding. The jeans that Ma Terrie wore today were a reward.

Ma Terrie had protected Madam from Honourable's backhand. Ma Terrie had stepped in just in time before the hand landed on her backside.

Ma Terrie had a wonderful asset for tying the loincloth and dancing. Ma Terrie was on the 'L' size but her backside was more of a 'XXL' size; an asset for dancing many traditional dances. Ma Terrie was a beauty at her age, very agile, and mothered the children. Madam had been mad at the revelations that Honourable had fathered yet another child with another woman. It was gossip from her trusted friend Bella. Ma Terrie had confirmed the rumour. Madam was mad at Honourable. The Children were also mad at him, but also at other things too.

They were growing up, and Mumene was becoming more socially conscious about her place in society; it worried her. Mumene, Sahara and Afrika knew there was something not quite right with the wealth distribution among their people. They realised the value of money, and how children could be left behind not because of their intellect but because of the family's social status. After high school, to get into the course of your choice at university, academic achievement was everything. But financial resources were key to moving forward. Her parents had dreamed of Mumene getting into Medicine or Law. It was an utopian vision. Ma Terrie thought of university as a dreamland. No one in her family had ever been to university. They learned trades and were good with their hands. They were happy. What she did not realise was that, Afrika, from an early age had exposure to another world. But something often bothered Afrika: her paternity.

Mumene had everything but bothered about the world around her. Mumene was an heir, and her father's selected next of kin. Mumene and Afrika had a shared passion for social justice. They bonded on that. Strangers had remarked about their closeness, especially considering their very different backgrounds; if they only knew.

It had happened the day Madam went to her regular Akirteh group. The only place, she had contact with women outside of Betsie, Bella and Marie-Noelle. The Akirteh group, was a must for most women irrespective of their social status. Honourable knew the Akirteh times and how long they went for; usually for three to four hours.

On that day, Ma Terrie walked into Honourable's bedroom to clean as usual. On this occasion, he was there, half dressed.

Ma Terrie had knocked and opened the door, as she would.

'Sorry Saar, I shall come back when you are dressed.'

'No Terrie, come in, do what you are doing.'

'Okay... Saar...Put something around your waist ...first Saar.'

'Terrie, what are you afraid of. Madam is gone to her Akirteh. How did you think she got here?'

Honourable said as he walked towards her. He shut the door and turned the key. Motionless, Ma Terrie watched as his penis enlarged. He pushed himself against her, softly. She could hear every breathe and heartbeat. Then he took her hand, and gently, he placed it over his penis. Holding her, he then motioned her to walk with him across the room into his bed. She obliged.

He pulled down her underwear and climbed on her. As she lay on her back, wondering whether to scream, he inserted his enlarged penis into her vagina. As he thrusted in and out of her quickly, he suddenly tried to pull out his penis so he could ejaculate outside of her. It was late, very late, actually. It was all over in a few minutes.

Ma Terrie, would miss her period that month. But was it Akornde, her on and off sex acquaintance, or was it

…Honourable? It happened once; neither of them spoke of it ever again. It was as if it did not happen.

As Afrika grew older, the resemblance between her and Mumene became local gossip. With no DNA tests, facial characteristics and resemblance was all they could go by. Even Bella and Betsie openly remarked on the resemblance between the two girls, just to call their friend's attention to it.

'No, not with Ma Terrie. I know Honourable has his way with women, but my dears, you are only imagining it. You are wrong this time.' That was Madam's response to her friends, when they spoke of the resemblance and the bond between the two girls. They never spoke of it to her again; they did not want to upset her. Madam on her part, never asked her husband nor Ma Terrie about Afrika's paternity. *It's not my business!* She assured herself.

Was Madam too afraid to know the truth?

CHAPTER 15

The Akirteh group

S ahara sought solace with her friends.

'Afrika, I must get off the phone now and take over the children, and then take Ahbotta to the elder's Akirteh group.'

'That's important; I knew that group keeps her sane.'

'I Agree. Akirteh provides these women the chance to discuss personal and health issues, social and cultural messages, failures and successes. As Ahbotta put it, Akirteh 'kept them alive and sound.'

'They can all share their worries about their children and grandchildren together. At Akirteh they worry aloud, you do not have to hold the messages in your head.'

'Bye now.'

'Bye Sahara.'

Ahbotta was not late. As she sat down, Manyibefour had the floor.

'We realised; we all shared the same concerns and aspirations for our children and their children, though we came from so many countries from the mother continent. My daughter is home without a job; my son and his wife are both jobless, but they all have those papers they call degrees. They went to school for a long time. My mother never went to school. She couldn't even read her name if it was written on that wall, in capital letters. But we did, these children also did. I saw them staying up very late reading books. They will say they are preparing for exams. My other nephew, you know him, Ahbotta, the mechanic you saw me with, works only for three days but would like to work for the whole week. Let me stop here, you have heard me; let another person speak.'

As a child, Manyibefour had worked on the farm like her ancestors before her. They lived in a big compound with members of the extended family. There was always something to do. Her ancestors tilled the land, but her parents ensured that she and her siblings had a good education. Her children, she would lament, 'will never understand how good it feels when you pull out a carrot from the earth and eat; when you climb a tree and pick the mangoes, sit on one of the branches and just savour them.' Her family were content, and happy, and joked about how wonderful life was. 'War, minerals, resources, I curse them, and those who rule the souls of those who worship those things!' Such thoughts were not always far away from the minds of these elderly women: 'We have seen our husbands, sons, neighbours die senseless deaths because of those things in the ground.'

Today I live on the thirteenth floor of a tall grey building in Melbourne. I spend afternoons sipping coffee in my apartment with other neighbours and friends. My hair has greyed. I am an old woman now. Back then, we had little money, little of everything but we were free. My flat overlooks a main road; it's nice, and I have my friends, old ones like me. We spend a great deal of time gossiping about the young girls when they come and go. We see them from the top but they cannot see us. How far apart could our lives be? Manyibefour thought to herself.

These old women and aunties 'put an eye' on the youth. Just what the girls' families want is just what the girls detest. They love the modern but have also kept the old ways.

The women would peep through the windows of their flats to check who may have been dropped off; they check the type of car. Was it an expensive car? What suburb? What was the racial background of the driver?

Not so much of a problem for the boys. They always have their freedom.

As for the girls, they would not have dreamt of sitting in a car alone with a male who was not their father, brother or husband. 'The children of today!' Ahbotta said, after she saw a girl, through her window kissing a male who had come to drop her off. Ahbotta, shook her head regretfully and groaned. At such moments, she would have flashbacks of her own life, and as a girl. She never forgot that first night with Atonga. Then there was the friend at the Akirteh group, Nyadirr.

Nyadirr was lucky with her two daughters. They had finished Law and Engineering at some of Australia's prestigious universities. They were both practicing at firms in North Melbourne and St Kilda respectively. Her sister-in-law, Amina, who used to be a Magistrate in Chantreville, was not so lucky. They are of similar age and migrated together two decades ago. Nyadirr's sister-in-law was now working in the community kitchen. She led a group of other women in teaching their daughters traditional cooking skills.

Amina will tell her friends, 'How did I move from the law court, to the kitchen? It's good, but, I'd rather sit on the bench. I studied for many years; I worked hard until that war.

I wish you my friends had met me in person while in Chantreville.'

Some of the members of the Akirteh had heard of Amina's past, 'the woman with the sharp tongue, smart as a whip and cunning as a tortoise.' She never lost a case. She saved the lives of many woman and prevented many child marriages. She was loved and admired. She was a good woman, yet as tough as elephant skin. As a lawyer, her male counterparts feared but revered her. She was smart and beautiful and used both qualities accordingly. Today, on impulse she shared some of her life stories with fellow women at Akirteh. It happened inadvertently and she spoke from the heart. These spontaneous moments were not uncommon among these women. This was their safe space.

It had been hard for Manyibefour to meet a man who could match her intellect and stand her outgoing and audacious nature. Samuel, her husband, did Medicine and graduated as a top student in his final year. That was 1970. They met at student camp; he was struck by her independence and personality. She filled the room when she walked in. This had kept many possible suitors away. It was the opposite for Samuel. He was besotted the moment he saw Manyibefour. Not the same with her.

Samuel and Manyibefour would learn that, their respective families had affianced them to the children of their respective family friends.

'Ruth is a local girl Samuel. Ruth is a good girl; quiet, obedient, submissive and would make a good wife. Her mother and grandmother both have co-wives and are happy with their respective co-wives. She would make a good mother. Samuel, you could go out and be the man. Ruth will be dutiful. She is very obedient. We have been watching her.' That was Samuel's mother's perspective for who would make a good wife for her son.

Ruth had lived only a few kilometres from Samuels's family. 'They were good people,' Samuel's mother advised her son. 'Her mother and I were childhood friends, my son. We both married the men our families selected.'

These women wanted the same for their children. Samuel's mother knew Ruth's family history going back generations. They were confident there was no bad blood in either of the families, a systematic background check, unwritten but known rules that families practice before any marriages are entered into. Samuel's family was besotted with Ruth. His mother saw her as the other daughter to add to her own brood.

Samuel fell for Manyibefour the moment he set eyes on her. She was extroverted, articulate, sharp and disobedient. Disobedient because she questioned the world, she had opinions of her own; a quality he wanted in a wife. *What a relief, another inquiring mind!* Samuel thought after meeting and listening to Manyibefour for the first time. *I think I have found the woman for me;* he told himself.

During the final year of university, Samuel's family started preparing for his wedding to Ruth.

'Mother, I know you want me to marry Ruth. It's true, I want a wife, a partner and someone to share my life with, someone to talk to. Ruth is everything but not that person, mother. I need a woman with an opinion, not a servant. I have seen the way you and Papa live, that's not what I want. It was good for you, but not for my generation.' Samuel's head remained bowed as he spoke to his mother softly but firmly. 'Mother, I am a man. I know what I want. Forgive me Yaya. I love another woman. I met her at university.' At this point tears streamed down his eyes. He mumbled some words to himself. He knew what might follow. 'I love you, but I am a man now.'

It was as if he had committed the worst crime against mother earth. As his mother put it, 'you are going astray. Marrying a book woman, is a life sentence; an immense blunder, Samuel. The woman's eyes are too open, Samuel. She will never obey you, they do not follow the culture. Women who go to school that far, do not listen and are not submissive, enough. Oh, what has school done to my son, the eye of the family! These book women are too free! Samuel, I am your mother; you are marrying Ruth!'

'Mother, I said I am sorry; if you want Ruth, you can marry her. I want a wife, not a servant.'

As if Samuel had slaughtered someone, his mother went into mourning for many months. She turned her back on him; she would not speak to him directly. He was heartbroken, but he knew the woman he wanted to live with. His desires, and what he wanted in a wife, were the exact opposite of what his mother and relatives wanted.

Samuel reflected over the months if he had made the right decision. *How I wished they had the same opportunities to know what I know and see what it was like to have a woman who could match one's intellect rather than focus on obedience and what was between the legs; sexual desires.* Samuel sobbed when he thought of his mother and his own sisters; he prayed that none of his nieces and nephews would ever tie the knot for those reasons, being the wishes of his mother. *Their thinking has to change and they should marry for happiness alone.*

It would take two long years for Samuel to finally gather the courage to express how he felt about Manyibefour to her. Samuel watched her send the boys packing, leaving them in tears too. He was a broken man between the two women who were all that mattered to him. Only one did not really know how he felt about her all this while. He had turned down the woman he had been betrothed at birth for her. *What if Manyibefour turned me down?* Samuel was worried.

After years of nurturing their friendship, Samuel finally had the courage to ask Manyibefour out for a date. When she accepted, he was elated. They kept their relationship a secret from their families for two years. When he finally opened up to his mother who was getting worried that he would never marry, it would take her another two years to agree to meet this book woman. *Two women who were the exact opposite of each other in many ways, but who one day had to live with each other. They were as stubborn as each other too.* Samuel was determined to be with his true love.

He must convince his mother that he was not making a mistake. This was the first girl in their hometown to go to university and to successfully finish a Health and Law degree. When he finally won her heart, he had to do it for his mother, win her heart to accept the woman he loved. 'It was like tying firewood on a dog's back; like climbing Everest.' It was hard work for two long years. His mother had the perfect idea of what a wife for

Samuel should look like. She had a wife for him, Ruth. 'Determination is key to success,' he kept reminding himself.

No one in the family could forget the first day Samuel's mother met Manyibefour. A scene had been expected. A scene it was too. Samuel had cautioned Manyibefour to expect a 'go away' reaction from his mother. Like all brides to be, she was to greet her future mother-in-law kneeling, not look her in the eyes, and keep her head bowed. Knowing Manyibefour, Samuel expected nothing more than a nod from her towards his mother. He had no problems with that and saw no reason why Manyibefour had to go down on her knees and through all the rituals. More so, towards other women, he did not mind. He detested all these old practices, he would question; 'why women are making things so much harder for other women?'

As they approached his parents' compound, one of the children who saw them walk up the hill ran ahead to announce their arrival. There were a few neighbours around rather than the extended family members as warranted by tradition. News of Samuel, their graduate son marrying a book woman had not impressed them. Those few family and neighbours who were there, came for curiosity rather than to welcome Manyibefour. As Manyibefour was introduced to the group, one after the other, Samuel's mother sat quietly, and watched. By tradition the bride-to-be had to greet the future mother-in-law last; all the respect was reserved for her. Manyibefour did the traditional three kisses on the cheek, while uttering a few words as she went around the semi- circle. As she approached Samuel's mother, she did not kneel, but instead went flat on her abdomen, and kissed her feet.

Samuel was aghast; his mother broke into tears, the neighbours in an absolute muddle. Good confusion!

Samuel's mother then rose to her feet, held Manyibefour's hand with her right hand and with the left hand motioned her to stand. She obeyed, head bowed. Samuel's mother wrapped her arms around Manyibefour, and these two women hugged for a long time. Samuel's mother raised Manyibefour's chin using her left hand and looked straight into her eyes. It was like long lost friends seeing each other after many years. Two strong willed women. Samuel's mother had been touched by Manyibefour's actions. Using her shawl, Samuel's mother dusted the dirt that was on Manyibefour's dress. No one had expected this from this book woman. Most young women had stopped the practice of going so low to their mother-in-law and resolved to kneel. They were modern women. Not only did Manyibefour respect the traditions, she had just revived a dying culture. This was only the beginning of the amazing qualities of this bride-to- be. She was a *culturzilla,* rather than the *bridezilla* that Samuel's mother had feared. After all, she was educated, but also cultured.

Within an hour, the news spread around the town like wildfire; word of mouth was their way of life. The members of the extended family all streamed in. This act of respect took everyone by surprise. Within a day, it was being talked about in neighbouring villages. If anyone had thoughts about education meaning the loss of their cultures, well, this was their evidence to the contrary. Samuel's mother became the one who led the charge for her other sons to marry for love and book women too. This was the beginning of how educated women were viewed favourably in this community.

Manyibefour gave birth to five children; she cooked and served meals at home, worked hard but never complained. That was four decades ago. Life was good until they had to leave and run for their lives.

She had sent one of the politician's sons to jail for the rape of a young student. She sentenced him to five years of hard labour with no parole period. This act of law and order was the beginning of her nightmares. She had no regrets for providing justice to an innocent girl. There were threats to her life following the sentencing. It was the first case where a man had been jailed for rape. The girls were always blamed for bringing it to themselves. In her sentencing she said, 'the rapist must pay for their crimes.'

Manyibefour and her family fled, when war broke out subsequently. They could have stayed, but with her professional status, she knew she had many enemies and had to be safe, at least for her children.

When Ahbotta heard this story at the Akirteh group, she was a changed woman. It changed her, and she stopped scouting for a wife for Johnny.

Australia accepted Manyibefour's family on humanitarian grounds. Manyibefour and her family, including her then very frail mother-in-law, moved into a high-rise flat in inner Melbourne. They enjoyed the freedom that Australia afforded them. With limited English, but with her legal skills, Manyibefour enrolled in a language class. She knew it was only a matter of time before she could practice law again. She would enrol in a local university, up-skill, and familiarise herself with the laws of her new country, then get back to practice as soon as she could. She itched to enter the job market as weeks went by, then months, then years. She started applying for clerical positions. Nothing fruitful came of it. A decade later she was simply referred to as one of the refugees. She was an Australian citizen. 'Refugee has become a badge of honour,' she would tell members of the Akirteh group.

Manyibefour detested such an honour badge at first but had no choice. She wondered what went wrong. Samuel struggled to have his medical degree recognised. To support his family, he started driving a taxi. As a political refugee, Samuel was unable to return to his homeland when peace came. He worked long hours but barely made ends meet.

Samuel applied for many jobs. The rejection letters he received were almost identical. They always started with how great his application was, but how there were better candidates. They wished him well for his next application. Samuel had received scores of such letters. Samuel fell into despair. He felt that he had lost his authority and manhood. He succumbed at the end. Samuel committed suicide after being repeatedly turned down for jobs. Manyibefour was left to raise their children as a widow.

Manyibefour had the Akirteh group to help keep her sanity. It was her support network. The women 'said it aloud' at Akirteh. *This biweekly gathering is a safe space for our stories. Women shared their stories.*

'I loved Australia for this possibility. People like myself could share similar quarters with people of other social spheres, but I lament not being given the opportunity to use my skills, to contribute to a society I want to give back to. Samuel worked hard for his degree but could not use his skills. He died a broken man,' Manyibefour sniffled as she shared these words with her friends at her Akirteh group.

The stories of these women were different but similar. They resonated with each other. They do not want the next generation to be left behind.

CHAPTER 16

Premarital Sex

Amara cleared her throat, stooped and clapped three times. Silence immediately filled the room, with all eyes directed at her. Amara cleared her throat again, then she spoke. 'I hope you all arrived in good health.'

The women responded to the greeting then she continued.

'My grandnephew Akut is twenty-one years old. Akut was born in Australia, shortly after his parents arrived from Zenyi. They were a proud mixed couple, both parents from the same country but from different tribes. A trained auto mechanic, Akut had a strict upbringing. His parents were gentle and loving. They had endured a lot in life, publicly shamed in the market square, after being caught in the 'act'. His parents, who had escaped a war, had lived in inhumane conditions in another country. They lived in slave-like conditions. They successfully walked for days and arrived in another camp, this time in Zenyi. The conditions were better but never like home. Akut for the first time went to school and learnt English and Swahili. He learnt to speak the native dialect where his family settled. He also spoke his mother tongue with his own parents. With the help of kind hearted neighbours, they successfully immigrated to Australia as refugees following many years of protracted circumstances in the refugee camps in Zenyi.

Akut's father, an Akar man, had married a Namdie girl. They were not your traditional couple. Most tribes did not intermarry. Amara always said to her children 'that marriage is a contract between families, not individuals'.

Akut's parents spoke limited English on arrival in Australia but brought with them a rich culture and their resilience. Madita and Amina were very enterprising; they having survived the harshness of war and displacement. Their marriage had been unconventional. It also started under strange circumstances too.

Madita and Amina met in a refugee camp. It was a difficult situation, because back in their homeland, their two tribes were at each other's throats. Kids are innocent and, in the camp, these children only saw themselves as youth. After a few years walking past each other, they became *friends*. They walked daily with the others after school to fetch water. Sometimes they would play, hide and seek. In the course of playing hide and seek, Madita touched Amina, accidentally. No words were spoken by the two of them, between each other, though they walked to the stream with the others. Then Madita on one occasion suggested they meet and speak about the *touch*. They did, and where they sat in an abandoned old house that became their private spot. At their usual spot at a planned time, Madita asked Amina to show him the colour of her underwear. She did, but everything then happened very quickly. Amina screeched, and it happened that someone was walking past. It was an old man who had been walking past but it was 4:00pm, bright daylight. He listened carefully as he struggled with his hearing. It was a human voice. *But this was hidden from everyone else.*

As curious as a cat, he peered into the hut through a small hole in the door. The abandoned hut was half standing and half on the ground, inside were Madita and Amina. 'It was consensual! She wanted it!' Madita told the old man who had asked him nothing.

They had been caught having sex; caught in the act by one of the uncles. Madita and Amina were half dressed from the waist up. As they tried to hurriedly pull up their pants, the old man stumbled inside, yet with a firm grip, held each of them tightly. He was a former local boxing champion and had a reputation for strength, despite his age. The old man was more embarrassed than the twosome. He pulled them out of the hut. Both were visibly shaking, frightened, heads bowed. Tears rolled down Amina's face; Madita was emotionless, and he went along as he was led. He resigned his fate to the old man and the community. This was a first in this place among the youth, how could this happen? 'Children these days want to taste the sweet corn before it is ready.' They were not ready for this, and this was premature. The old man fumed, tightened his grip and took the pair directly to Madita's parents' hut within the camp. He did not have to finish his story before the decision was agreed upon.

'Madita did wrong; and Amina - stupid, very stupid. How could you have done this to us? Madita, how are we going to fix this with her family? Where are we going to get the dowry? What were you two thinking? Some man would have paid dowry, only to find nothing there, no blood on his bed, after his first night. See the shame you have brought our family?' Madita's mother and father rebuked.

Madita's parents had to get the number of cows warranted for such a 'crime' ready within two new moons.

During this waiting period, Amina had to live with her paternal aunt, Amaratou, the family's matriarch.

Amaratou decided on important family matters like this. Amaratou was the eldest daughter of the family, and her father doubled up as the local chief for their clan. Her word was final. Her brothers and male relatives would debate for hours, deciding the number of cattle for every girl in the family. There was no time limit, the time it took was they time they used. Brides were priced for their 'beauty and intellect'. The number of cows and gifts were a direct *symbol* of her standing within the community, her self-respect and that of her family. The men would negotiate endlessly; the final decision was Amaratou's, the matriarch of the family. That's how Akut's parents Madita and Amina got married.

Amaratou the seasoned orator, made the decision. As the first princess born to her father and the eldest of his forty- five children, she was next to him in decision-making, even if a son would later ascend the throne.

Her father had married five women. He was a respected herdsman, Amaratou's father worked hard. The local men desired him as an in-law. His status would inevitable 'rub off' onto them and their families. Marriage provided them with such possibilities by direct links to the noble man and his family. His last two wives had been gifts from his friends.

Marriage was and still is regarded as a social insurance policy for women in many quarters. Children born to them within these relationships strengthen that. Motherhood is not only desired; it was almost mandatory. Premarital sex reduced the possibility of a good suitor, therefore of secure and life insurance. Worse, if the girl became pregnant, out of wedlock; the prospects for her and her unborn children were precarious. It was said that there was some level of altruism and informal welfare in arranged marriages.

Amaratou the princess was tall and slender with blue ebony skin. She wore tribal amulets around her ankles, wrists and waist, with tribal marks engraved on her forehead and cheeks. Her ancestors had carried these marks, so too are her children; but not her grandchildren. The horizontal lines on her forehead were her tribe's totems. From the totems on a child's face or body, you could tell where the child was from and who her people were, even if they were 300km away. This was the system that elders used to identify and return lost children. It was one's identity and the tribespeople carried these totems with pride.

Amaratou had her front upper teeth extracted at age twelve; a cultural practice amongst her tribespeople. As she struggled to eat the pieces of meat on her plate, at Akirteh, she knew she had made the right decision for her grandchildren, not to have their front teeth extracted. She complained how difficult it was to chew without teeth but recalled with pride the day her teeth had been extracted. She loved her tribe and heritage but she thought, there were practices such as the teeth extraction that they could do without. She ensured that none of her grandchildren had their teeth extracted.

Amara went on, 'Akut, loved work, but work was hard to find. The boy had a rough time when he left school in year eleven. His teachers had told him to aim for technical school, despite his intention to go to university. The others dissociated him from social activities. He was unable to afford the normal things that others could afford. Life was tough at home too. Amina and Madita finally separated after many years, after being paraded naked.

Amina had a job, and Madita felt he could no longer control Amina. He was left with the responsibility of caring for the children; Akut was the eldest child and with that came more responsibilities. Things became harder by the day, at home and at school.

Amina made the decision to leave the family home. Amina and Madita had to decide what was best for them and their children. They had thought they were in love at the time their families ordered their marriage. Amina now a hairdresser, took their three daughters, and the father stayed with the boys in the family home. They were both loving parents towards their kids, but circumstances had changed. Neither of them was forty years old yet.

Akut took on a lot of responsibility. His grades dropped at school. The teachers did not understand what was happening at home. He kept everything a secret. He had been brought up to keep family matters under the roof, 'a house without disagreements is a house without people.' Theirs was a house with people, thus there were bound to be disagreements.

Akut left school, but under the guidance of an uncle, from his community, went on to complete an apprenticeship. He studied hard at his local TAFE, and upon completion expected to find a job. Six months passed, twelve months, eighteen months, and now two years. His family did not have enough money to open a motor mechanic garage for him but thought Akut may benefit from the guidance of another mechanic. Things were difficult; Akut struggled to cope. All the cards seemed to be lined up against Akut. But Akut was not giving up easily.

Amara, now the matriarch, was steadfast with support. A friend at Akirteh offered to speak to her cousin, a mechanic, about the possibility of taking Akut in as an apprentice. This network opened a door and Akut started work there. He worked three days weekly. Through Akirteh, relationships are formed and opportunities created. Akut was an indirect beneficiary of Akirteh. I thank you all for listening.' Amara stooped and with three claps ended her conversation.

Today, the Akirteh was struggling financially. The women could not provide the required evaluation necessary for future funding. They had to show evidence of the need for this group, and benefits of the group to their families. Amara, Ahbotta, Manyibefour and other members planned to visit their local member of parliament to discuss the situation. Individually, they could not; as a group they felt stronger.

The story of Akirteh is not uncommon. Akut wanted more work and remains hopeful to one day own his own garage and go to university to complete a degree. Amara is optimistic about her Akirteh, but they never forget where they hailed from. At the Akirteh group, Ahbotta and fellow members had a safe space to reminisce about Muka and their respective places of birth. It provided a space to connect and to share life stories. Akirteh healed these women from within. It was an opportunity to take a break from everyday events; even from Ahbotta's beloved Sahara and her family. It was her space and she shared it with women close to her age.

CHAPTER 17

Communal discipline

After the previous day at Akirteh, Ahbotta was more determined to share the stories of her childhood, homeland and cultures with her grandchildren and family. They have heard her repeat this, many times: 'I want them to know the way of my people, so they never forget their place and person.'

'Ahbotta, they are too young to understand.'

'Johnny, they will remember what they can when I am no longer here.'

'As a child, we spent a lot of time running around the village. The Bororos (Fulani people) herded the cattle and lived what we thought were isolated lives on the far away hills. In those days we had no pads and phones and all those things you know.'

'What are pads, Ahbotta?'

'Go away from here Johnny, I know you are mocking me that I do not know the names of all those things you touch with your fingers.' Johnny never ceased joking with his mother.

'Ahbotta, the children are all here waiting for you to start,' Sahara interjected.

They sat on the rug as they often did, listening to Ahbotta. They would interrupt occasionally, though, often at the least appropriate times.

'Ahbotta, I am interested in the life of the Bororo people back there. I read a book most recently that mentioned them in passing, but I know you have spoken about them on occasions.'

'So, you are ready to listen to me now?'

'Ahbotta, I am sitting here. Sahara, join us when you are ready. We are in Ahbotta Storyland.' Johnny added cynically.

'Children, are you ready?'

'Yes Ahbotta,' they all responded together.

'Once upon a time there was a place called Muka located in the grasslands of a small country in the west of the African savannah region. It had beautiful lakes, the vegetation was evergreen and produce was bountiful. The locals lived harmoniously, and the *Bororos* lived in harmony with the land on the rolling hills that were very far away. Muka could easily be christened the Vegetable Village, because of all the fresh garden produce that the farmers grew.

Truckloads of their produce were exported to neighbouring countries. Tea, coffee, groundnuts beans, corn, cassava, coco-yams, plantains, bananas, potatoes, pumpkins, carrots, cucumbers, parsley, celery-name it, they all grow happily together in Muka. The Bororos owned most of the livestock.'

'Ahbotta, I'm keen to hear more about these people,' Johnny interrupted.

The Bororos are a nomadic people; they have a wandering yet sustainable existence. They live in harmony with the environment. They live on the hills with their animals: cows, goats, horses, sheep and chicken. They get their milk from the cows and goats, eggs from chicken, meat from cows and goats, and protein supply is bountiful. Families sell some of their produce to buy grains such as maize and rice, and groundnuts, and vegetables that are part of their staple diet, from the local farmers. Men farm and guard the livestock: women stay home to look after the homestead and raise the children.

The Bororos are devout Muslims; their prayer mats are ever close to them. Interdependence is a way of life that they all celebrate. One could easily mistake a family visit to a sick person at the local health centre to a tribal trip, simply because of the utter number of guests. Such social support is integral for the survival of this group who live an almost exclusive lifestyle. Thanks to modern technology, 'as the times have changed people have changed.' Cultures evolve, and the Bororos have evolved too. When one watches these people, it affirms the saying that 'man made culture but when man and society evolve, the culture must evolve with them.'

'Intermarriage, previously uncommon is now a reality among the Bororos and their host communities. In this society, not limited to the Bororos, polygamy (polygyny) is common. A man and co-wives living together, nonetheless detested by many, the practice remains common.

For the sick, there are always guests to support you through the journey; good acts from a close-knit community. The Bororos would stop and pray anywhere whenever it was prayer time. During Ramadan celebrations, the women dress in colourful clothing, with nicely braided cornrows. The word 'prettiness' was synonymous with these

Bororo women, notwithstanding their isolated existence from the wider community. The Bororos are considered a peaceful group who will stand up for themselves if pushed.

Disputes with local farmers were common, particularly when their cattle destroy or eat farmers produce. Lawsuits, if not resolved at the community level with local chiefs, could end up in the customary courts or other law jurisdiction.

Child marriages were once considered a norm for the Bororos, but not for much longer. The children were kept home and girls were groomed for marriage from an early age. Betrothing children was common back then. As children we were curious what it was like to live like the Bororos. We lived only a few kilometres away yet we were so far away.

The few women, who ventured away from their homes often, did so in groups. The Bororos were good walkers too, travelling very long distances on foot, often with load on the head. They had horses, but I do not recall seeing a woman on any of the horses. Women made money through the sale of fresh yoghurt, milk and butter.

They would carry large bowls on their heads with their produce. The bowls were always well protected from the heat of the sun and always very clean. The Bororos intrigued people's imagination, and to date remain a mystery. The women were slender; they wore colourful jewellery and often homemade makeup. Lime greens, red and yellow are colours you would associate with their clothing, bright and brighter indeed.

As children, we wondered why such colours. Unfortunately, the lines of communication between the Bororos and locals were almost non-existent, just as the person-to-person contact hardly existed. Maybe it did among the adults, but not with the children. Probably the Bororos had similar imaginations about their locals too, who only ever referred to the women as '*Mamiemyiah*' and men as '*Malam.*'

For the polygamist household, the eldest wife led the brood, as custom dictated, she being the *head mother* and the *head wife*. A new wife strengthened the status of the husband in the community. That was then. Many wives were a demonstration of the man's prowess and his manhood within his community.

Large families brought such perceived influence; peers and the locals often admired such men. Not sure if the women did. .

Every wife had a hut of her own where she lived with her children. It was not uncommon for the children of one wife to spend more time in their other 'mothers' houses. The husband's house was always strategically built at the entrance or at the heart of the compound. Compounds are often built in a U shape or semi-circle, with the main house in the compound positioned at the bottom of the U, visible to guests as they approached. A low fence not higher than a metre made from local materials sometimes surrounded the homestead.

Animals had a special place within the homestead. They formed the primary source of income for the family's livelihood. The young males tended the animals; occasionally girls will join their brothers, though girls' primary role was to assist their mothers in the home. School attendance was simply a faraway dream for these children.

Muka was one of the few villages around that had pipe borne water in the 1970's, not piped by government but by the locals. The Muka children grew up drinking 'pipe' water from the taps, not the 'water' you see on TV adverts these days used by some as bait to entice donors to donations to their charity.'

Sahara interrupted. 'It saddens the heart that children must drink such water and also that a child's face will appear on international TV to raise funds. Aren't there better ways to ask for sponsorships?'

Ahbotta then continued. 'There were times that an explanation could not be given why the taps would not flow for weeks. This did not bother the local children; they did not understand why then. As a grown-up now, I know. The pipes and water tanks were probably being cleaned or some machinery required replacement and had to be imported from abroad. For kids these were happy times, they could see their friends more often after school and could all play together on their way to collect water?'

'Ahbotta, did you play games with your friends?' asked Njinwi.

'But Ahbotta is old, how could she run around and play?' added Fonnwi.

Everyone laughed as hard as they could.

'I was once a child just like you,' smiled Ahbotta.

The boys could not imagine their grandmother as a child. They laughed even harder. Ahbotta simply continued, as she basked in the moment.

'It was an opportunity to walk together with other children to the local stream about half a kilometre away to fetch water. The village children would play games on the way. We sometimes kept our mothers waiting and wondering what we were up to. Sometimes the water was needed to prepare the main evening meal for the family. Fetching water was a good chore. We would play with our friends. There was a game called tabalah, a version of hopscotch. The children loved it and there was a girl by the name of Lucy who was so good at tabalah. The children always wanted Lucy on their team.

Sizooh, was another game the girls loved playing. A stretchy rubber or elastic was required for sizooh. The girls would pull one out of a nice dress, or their brothers would carve thin rubber from tyre tubing for their sisters if you were lucky. This was the ultimate play gear for sizooh; the tyre tubing stretches well, the most important item for this game.

Other games children played on the way to the stream were dodge ball. Children divided themselves into two teams with one player inside the ring. There were those who were good at aiming and those good at dodging the ball. You never wanted them on the same team because the other team will not get a turn before their mothers' screaming voices started calling for us to bring the water.'

'Were there no games for the boys, Ahbotta?' one of the boys asked.

'That's where I was going next, Fonnwi. The boys played Bizerte, a game with marbles. Football was the king of games and they played with each other at every opportunity. Anything round and soft could be used as a ball, including even plastic bags tied firmly together. The boys were more at liberty compared to girls to go out and play. They were not watched over like a mother hen over the chicks, unlike girls who were like their mothers' and aunties' chicks. As the children played their respective games, suddenly they would hear loud echoes. It was not an echo, it was always one of the mothers' voices. My mother had a loud voice.'

'Just like yours,' Johnny said with smile.

'Metti! Metti! Metti! That was my mother shouting at the top of her voice calling for me. 'I

NEED THAT WATER to add into the pot that I have on the fire cooking NOW! THE POT IS BURNING! That was often followed by a series of questions and threats. Then, there was the next scream from a mother from the next compound, the next, and the next. The messages were maybe different but all similar like the tones in their voices. The children did not have to be told what awaited them at home upon their return.'

'Did your mummy make you sit in the naughty corner, Ahbotta?' came a small soft voice from Chenwi.

'Oh no! back then; there were no naughty corners. There were big smacks with a stick.'

'You mean your mummy hurt you with a stick? That's really mean!'

Ahbotta did not respond to the remark, instead she continued.

'When the children heard their mothers' voices calling, they would suddenly realise they had forgotten all about the water fetching errand. The buckets and jars were often still empty. The children were often nowhere near the stream or pond. As the voices of parents echoed, we would hurriedly collect the water jugs and sprint like antelopes. It was sometimes too late for those teams that had not had their turn. For the boys, that could mean missing the chance to equalize that goal.

The screams between teams and those from the mothers were like music in the air and would cancel out each other. With drums one could start 'dancing' to their music, but only if you could bear any of the mothers, like Yaya Sineh who had the stature of a military commander and a backside to match. Though she was not a fast runner, when she had grip of you, you paid the price for everyone else. Sometimes it would be too late, because one of the mothers would have caught up with the children. They could creep in quietly without anyone noticing them and when that happened, one unfortunate soul was in for everyone else's disobedience.

The community perceived that the child belonged to everyone and they all had a responsibility to right any wrongs if they came across any unruly children without fear of retribution from their families. Parents corrected any child who was considered not to be of good demeanour. There were the unwritten rules where people celebrated the birth of a child, showed up for the naming ceremonies, for baptisms and dedications, for First Holy Communion and other important family gatherings, including weddings. Everyone celebrated success or stepped in and shared the burden when a family was grief stricken such as with the death of a family member. These unwritten rules transferred to discipline too.

On one fateful day as we played, Ma Sineh, quietly crept in without any of us noticing her presence. We must have been over engaged with the game we were playing.

She gripped two of the girls and knocked their heads together.

One freed her hand and disappeared into the bushes.

The other was not so fortunate. Ma Sineh had firm grip of her hand. 'Please let me go, I will get the water now,' the poor little girl screamed between her tears. You should have been home by now. I heard your mother's voice a few times while sitting in my kitchen. You ignored her calls. You can't ignore me now.'

Ma Sineh turned around and just behind her was a big stick.

'Tap, tap, tap, fell the stick on the girl's backside as she screamed her lungs out.'

'Please, please help me!' she shouted, but all her friends had disappeared, she was alone. Her friends were peering from a distance. They felt sorry for her because she was the scapegoat today and was receiving the punishment of everyone else.'

'Did she stop hurting her, Ahbotta?' came another little voice from Bihnwi.

'No, Ma Sineh took her home straight to the little girl's mother who was waiting outside their tiny hut with a whip in her hand. Her mother was fuming with anger when she saw the little girl. 'Thank you for bringing her, Ma Sineh; I hope you taught her a good lesson. This child has changed. She has joined a very bad group of friends.' Her mother uttered these words, sighed with relief before thrashing her as well. Luckily her father was not home, she would have received her third punishment.'

The grandchildren at this point were almost all crying.

'I feel so sorry for the little girl, Ahbotta. They are so mean!' cried Fonnwi.

'How cruel could those people be?' Johnny said with anger in his voice.

'My son, we endured a lot as children. They called it discipline back then.'

'That's not discipline Ahbotta, that is outright abuse of children. Where were these children's rights?' asked Njinwi. 'Rights back then?' Ahbotta asked. 'What rights, chicken rights?'

Sahara sighed; the expression on her face was obvious; no child deserved such punishment.

'Back then they thought it was a good thing, now we know you can discipline children differently; use naughty corners or take away the electronic devices.'

Everyone sighed as they stood up and stretched their limbs.

'That was a sad story, Ahbotta,' the twin boys said pitifully.

'Come my child, I will never use a whip on any of you. I will never let anyone do that to you. I received lashes for all of us when I was a child. That was enough to go around,' Ahbotta reassured her grandchildren as they all gathered around her.

'Things were different back then. If the parents were respected members of the community and considered to have high morals, this was also expected of their children. If their children were seen in any compromising situation, the punishment was often severe as they were 'bringing the family name into disrepute. The family name and honour were and still is everything.

Families, my children, lived together, worked together and pulled through life together. They supported the sick as one unit. Ma Sineh was one of those mothers known for her generosity and communal activities. This made her family prominent within the community and her children were expected to carry on with that 'tradition'. Village children could recognise Yaya Sineh's footsteps and would 'disappear' into thin air if they 'sniffed' her. Parents on the contrary loved her and would even threaten their children to bring them to her for disciplinary action if they did not change their unruly ways. No child or parent could mess around with Ma Sineh, not even the local rascals, my children.'

'I hate her, Ahbotta! Do not take me to her!' said the boys.

'I like the Bororos instead,' said Bihnwi.

'I would like to go back to Muka and see how things are today, Ahbotta,' added Sahara.

'I will come with you,' Johnny said as they all had one big hug.

CHAPTER 18

Piercing the thatch ceiling

Sahara pondered what life was all about as she contemplated on a big trip to Muka with her family. She wanted Afrika, Veronique and Mumene to be there when she went. *It will be better with the four of us together.* She also had other business to discuss with the girls first, so she picked up her phone to call Afrika first.

'Hello Afrika, is that you?'

'Hi Sahara, how are you? Really good.'

'Hope you are all well at home.'

'We are doing fine. The children are good. Ahbotta, and Johnny are all doing very well. Ahbotta, told us a moving childhood story recently that made me want to visit Muka and see how things are for myself.'

'What is it that will move you so much, you want to go there?'

'Just the important things in life. I'm not going immediately, but maybe during the second half of the year. You know, good and bad.'

'If it is during the holiday period, we could all plan and travel together. Let's speak to Mumene, and Veronique.'

'What a brilliant idea! But I must have that job first, so I can pay for the children. I want them to come too!'

'Well, you said your current manager is very different from everyone else you've worked for. What's his name again?'

'Mr Thomas Black, indeed he is, and he has taken affirmative action; he supervises his non-European born staff himself.'

'Not sure if that is a good thing or not!'

'I think, it is a good thing. He is for real, he likes competence and is very outcome driven.'

'That sounds good to me. I trust your judgment.'

'Same here!'

'Let's speak in a few days about this travel thing. But aren't you going away for work in a couple of days? When you return let's start the planning. In between, I shall speak to Mumene and Veronique.'

'Sounds like a plan.'

'Safe travels; bye for now, love you.'

'Thank you. Love you, Bye.'

Afrika, also working in a mining firm, agreed it was a good idea to visit Muka again, the four of them together.

Afrika was also thinking about her future, she contemplated about returning home permanently. *This trip with Sahara, Mumene and Veronique will help me decide.* As if she was dreaming, she took a deep breathe, slowly, then turned around and smiled to herself. She stared in the mirror next to her, immediately, she had a sudden sense of relief. *Life is different here. I don't know if it is better or worse. Let me travel back with those who know me best and collectively, we can make a decision.*

Back at work, looking at his organisation chart, Thomas, Sahara's boss observed that, all his senior executives were men, the *coloured* staff, regardless of gender were at the lower rungs of the organisation's ladder; they exited the organisation only after a few years of service, often too early to reach middle management. *I wonder why this happens? People seem nice. Now with the upcoming new vacancies I hope my middle management and senior leadership can start looking like our clients.* Thomas thought.

Mr Thomas Black, had been raised by his mother, and grandmother; now he lived with his wife, and their four daughters. He often bragged to his staff and friends about women; 'I know women; I have lived with them all my life.

Seven of them to be exact he would say, they boss me around, but get things done, I trust their abilities. I need women like them around this place; I mean within this company.'

After being informed the positions he wanted advertised, had been, Thomas told his assistant and HR Director, 'We need to appoint people from different cultural backgrounds other than our own into those leadership roles. We need women in there too!'

'But sir, we do not have any qualified women around from those backgrounds,' responded his HR Director.

'Go and **look** for them Mr. Pitt. Things must change; bring women of all colours and ages.'

Three weeks later Mr Black called Jenny, the PA into his office and invited his Director of Human

Resources, Mr. Pitt. 'Thank you, Jenny, Pitt and Patricia for coming,' he commenced.

'Not a problem Mr Black.' They replied.

'Patricia, how did you go with the short-listing of applicants? Remember we need diversity in this company and I mean, real diversity.'

'We have ensured that. I brought you the list as I thought you might want to see it! Have you had a chance to read your emails this morning? I sent you the soft copy.'

'Not really, thank you, Patricia.' He said as he adjusted himself on his chair, while rocking to and fro at the same time.

Pen in hand, looking very relaxed. He was everything the boss, you would say if you walked into his large office. Antique French chaise, marble table, you name it. The décor was exquisite and of good taste. The man appeared to be of noble background but loved the ordinary things in life too. He had charisma to go with it too.

Mr Black looked at the list handed to him, his eyes narrowed, lips pursed. He was tense.

'John, Peter, Susan, Mary, Catherine, Albert' he read the first names while checking the surnames at the same time... he stopped midway, turned looked at both women, and then he turned to Pitt.

'Did I not say I wanted diversity?'

'Yes, we have men and women as you can see.' Replied Pitt.

'Okay, so where is Ahmed, Najib, Amina, Deng, Bihnwi, Ngami, Amandeep, Lu, Li?' Didn't anyone with those sorts of names apply?' Asked Thomas, who appeared visibly frustrated, but not angry.

The two women starred at each other.

'We shortlisted the most appropriate candidates,' replied Patricia.

Upon hearing this, Mr Black turned to his staff sitting there.

'Why don't we reschedule this meeting in another three weeks? Send out another call for applications with the hope we could attract the APPROPRIATE candidates. I would like to see a mix. We shall have diversity here. It's no longer a choice; we need to have everyone here. Also send me the list of all applicants by email. I rely on you to provide me with a shortlist.'

After three weeks, Patricia returned with a list of names and résumés in a green folder.

'Hello Patricia, how did you go? Before we start, would you like a cup of tea, or coffee?'

Thomas was already walking to the corner of the room where he had the coffee machine. He liked to make his own coffees whenever possible.

'Oh yeah, will have one, no sugar please, Thomas.'

'Consider it done!' Thomas smiled as he turned around.

A few minutes later he returned with their coffees in hand.

'Where are the names you've decided on? I need to also see their résumés.'

'I have them here,' Patricia said, handing him the folder.

Unbeknown to Patricia, Thomas had also gone through the list of all applicants himself earlier and had a list of his own. He crosschecked his list with that of Patricia's and his HR team.

Of the 25 applicants only one name from Patricia's list featured on his. They had each shortlisted 10 candidates.

Thomas looked at Patricia in utter silence.

'Could you get Pitt in please?'

Patricia stepped out and returned some moments later with Pitt.

'Patricia and Pitt, I appreciate your efforts with this, take this, make a copy for me, schedule interviews for the first week of September. That's in two weeks with all these candidates. If they are all good, we can find roles for them elsewhere, across the organisation. If they are not 'APPROPRIATE', then we continue the search until we find the APPROPRIATE person. You must be quick with this; we need these positions filled. I'm confident these people want to work.'

They spent an hour together. The boss did the job of his Director, Manager and Assistant, with no hard feelings nor raised voice. Was this leadership by action?

'I shall attend all the interviews, Pitt.'

'That will be nice.' Pitt responded, as he nodded at the same time.

'Patricia, we shall interview all ten candidates on my list.

Block out two mornings for the interviews.'

The following week, the shortlisted applicants, filed through over two mornings; Amandeep,

Marjna, Sahara, John, Anawut, Michael, Mohamed, Mikaela, Anna Marie, Laura and Lopez.

Five were short listed again from this group for another round of interviews. Sahara, Laura, Mohamed, Amandeep and John made it to the second round.

Following the interviews, Patricia was tasked with the referee checks, the last step before offers were made to the three best candidates.

Two days later, Patricia, returned to her boss.

'Thomas, I have done the referee checks. I could not get through to Sahara and Mohamed's referees. I did speak to John, Amandeep and Laura's referees.

'I think I should get Peter and Anna who were in the first round of interviews. They would be perfect for the job,' Patricia suggested.

Mr Black, upon hearing this turned pink, then white. He was visibly upset, now. He even raised his voice and questioned her authority over him. Mr Black, opened the green folder and dialled the phones that Mohamed and Sahara had provided.

He dialled all numbers and for some reason the numbers for all of Sahara and Mohamed's four referees could not be reached.

'That's too bad. I thought they were excellent at the interview, that's why I wanted all five. Okay, let me see what I can do.'

Thomas went back into his computer, opened his email folder to see if there was anything he could do. *Why not check the numbers just in case*, Thomas thought to himself? To his amazement, all the numbers Patricia handed him were mixed up. Mr Black was furious but remained calm. *An error or a coincidence? Maybe the former.*

Calmly he went through all the phone numbers that had been provided by the candidates. All referees answered his calls.

Were the stars lined up for these candidates or against Patricia? Mr Black conducted all the referee checks himself. John, had not quite made the criteria in the strictest sense. The other two candidates had not only completed their degrees, they had work experience.

Black was furious, and he decided to go through all the recruitment records of senior staff within the company that had occurred during the previous eighteen months. Not only were unqualified people hired, none of their staff met the criteria for diversity.

After that he called Pitt into his office.

'Pitt, hire all four of them, but for John. *Their CVs are too good.* Replace John's name with Mirjana's and call her in for an interview as soon as possible. We shall create roles for all of them.'

Thomas Black decided to be the primary supervisor for all the new employees. He told Pitt, 'I want to nurture them to senior management roles. They will bring the diversity we need here. It's good for business. You only have to look at the evidence, Pitt. They will open new doors for us in places we could never imagine, because they know the people, the people know them, and some of them speak the same language, Pitt.'

Pitt, nodded in affirmation as Thomas spoke. He uttered no words.

Sahara under the leadership of Mr Black flourished. She confided this was the fourth time she had applied for a position in his company, 'some at very low levels' as she thought it would be difficult starting at a senior level. The others had similar stories to share.

Mr Black knew quality when he saw it; he was not wrong with Laura, Amandeep, Sahara and

Mohamed nor with Mirjana. Thomas Black believed in the fair go, an Australian way of life and fair go, he practiced. His grandparents had migrated some seventy years earlier. *I have the responsibility to include everyone; to make all of us feel we all have a place at the table and equal opportunities to reach there.* He often reminded himself.

Sahara became a senior manager in eighteen months. *I feel this is it, and I would give my best back to Mr Black for this opportunity.* Sahara promised herself.

Sahara had a vision, and such thoughts were never too far away from her mind. She waited for the day, someone like her was going to run one of the large multimillion dollar companies in the country. Sahara pushed the thoughts away from her mind, *well maybe someday.* She was now in her fifth year working under the supervision of Thomas Black. Mr Black was impressed with her attention to detail and her breath of industry knowledge. He gave Sahara and Laura the opportunity to act in several senior leadership positions.

Sahara shared her professional life experiences with Afrika and the others. They all celebrated the change and the new opportunities that had opened for Sahara. Sahara had endured a lot. She had even cleaned chicken feet to make ends meet. Now she was a director at this multinational firm. There was only one position between her and the national executive director. But there was no rule that said, she could not go straight to the top if the opportunity presented itself.

As Afrika laid in bed in her beautifully decorated inner- city apartment, she reflected on her day's work. *I have so much to do today and need to go in fresh and relaxed.*

Her alarm started ringing, it was 7:00am. The radio came on automatically, it doubled as an alarm clock. It was just in time, for the news. The radio was always in the background as she prepared for work in the mornings. Midway through the news, the word Sahara captured her attention, there was an interlude.

'The mother continent, now what has happened again? Who had seized power or refused to hand over around the Sub Saharan Region? *Oh, this mother!*

It was more than the usual news items from the continent. It was neither about Sub-Saharan Africa nor the Saharan desert. It was about a Ms Sahara.

During this second attempt, with the words Sahara Chebo, Afrika's eyes widened, ears in devotion. The announcer apologised for the technical error then continued. Sahara Chebo has been appointed as the new Chief Executive Director of the Alabakum Mining Group (AMG).

Afrika listened before she started to scream. 'How did this happen? How can this be? Finally!'

Meanwhile a series of questions went through Afrika's mind as she waited for more. Maybe there were more details to come, or nothing.

Is it real? Am I dreaming? How does she look like? What colour is her skin? What is the colour of her hair, long, blonde, brown, any extensions, any Brazilian or Indian hair?

That's her for you, always metamorphosing. Yes, this gives them the ability to be whoever they want. That is Sahara for you, a tall ebony beauty. To have an indication of what she looks simply ask Dr Google about ebony beauty; pull the images together and then try to pick one of them and see how difficult it is to come up with a number one. They all seem to be the first, irrespective of where they live or how long they were removed from their beloved continent during the transatlantic slave trade. Yes, that's the African queen for you.

Afrika, stopped and her mind returned to the announcement.

Afrika though, still entertained thoughts of the colour of the appointee to this new senior role. *Is this not the Sahara I know? I need to hear the full announcement again. I need more.*

Are Sahara's eyes blue, green, hazelnuts or brown like mine? And... and... and...? Too many questions Afrika, stop thinking, Afrika, chill. Sahara, Sahara, Sahara. These thoughts flew through her mind in succession of each other.

While the thoughts were going through her mind, Afrika started dancing. Standing at the same spot, she moved her hips from side to side, three times, and then twice from back to front in quick sudden movements.

She does this for about three minutes, stops, laughs loud and hard.

'At last, FINALLY,' at the top of her voice, while dancing around the beautiful lounge room.

Afrika stopped again suddenly, took a deep breathe, while she reflected at the same time. She had too many questions, but her emotions had clearly overtaken every nerve in her brain.

'Should I believe the radio? Is this not media? 'The stereotypes about US,' she said loudly to herself as she pointed at the same time to herself using both her index fingers. 'But you know there are some really good journalists out there who are never swayed by the politics of the day. They share a balance view; not like those who are only interested to get it out, rather than getting their facts right. What happened to journalism? Social media has taken over. True or false, it's who is out there with it first. Nonsense!'

The announcer apologised again for the technical error, with a gentle and resolved voice. The Press Release was read in its entirety.

Between the partial and the complete announcement, Afrika had messaged Mumene, Veronique and Sahara to tune in to the VSS National Radio.

"WHAT"! Afrika, screeched at the top of her voice, 'CEO, CEO this is unbelievable.'

She jumped up and down. She would not listen to the rest of the Press Release. The Alabakum Mining Company was one of the largest mining companies in the country and this was enough for Afrika that

Sahara was now in command. Afrika needed to know no more, she needed to hear no more.

Afrika cried, laughed and shouted. The mixed feelings of joy, surprise and disbelief, hit her in a single moment. Afrika also danced around her lounge room. 'Oh my God.' She grabbed her phone. Rang Sahara a few times but the number was engaged. She couldn't get through to her. *Others must have heard the announcement too,* she thought. With one quick thought, she decided to send a text message instead. She didn't want to be late for work. She sent the text message.

> 'My dearest Sahara,
> CONGRATULATIONS!
> I heard the announcement. My heart is filled with joy. I always believed in you. Despite what we have been through, your focus, capabilities and sincerity have finally shown through. Your appointment gives hope to many women, youth, children and others. Sahara, you may not know this, but you, I mean, you **Sahara**, just **Pierced the Thatch Ceiling!** Not the Glass Ceiling, not the Bamboo Ceiling, but

the Thatch Ceiling. I am proud of you and I am equally proud of Mr. T. Black!

Call me when you can. I'll try to call again, later.'

XOXOXOXOXOXOOXOXOXOOXOXOXOXOXOXO

Afrika.

Afrika, clicked send, then watched her mobile phone screen. It showed 'sending' for about five seconds, before 'sent' appeared. Those five seconds were like eternity. Speaking to herself, she asked, 'Sahara, Piercing the Thatch Ceiling?'

Now half dressed, she glanced at the clock as it ticked away. It seemed to be ticking faster than it normally would. *It did not matter today. They will understand when I explain what just happened this morning.*

She hurried and was almost running to her car.

Drive safely Afrika! She reminded herself.

Work was important, but for Afrika there was the added layer of her dignity and keeping her sanity. *I loathe any able- bodied person seen to be free loading. How does an able- bodied person make a choice to stay home and be fed? What about their families and children? Why immigrate in the first place? Make the decision to cross all the seas and oceans to stay at home and get fed? No, you lose your dignity and, in some instances, the community will make you lose your sanity simply for being welfare dependent. Welfare is a safety net; point, not a salary, don't be fooled.*

Afrika's mind kept returning to the announcement. *Sahara, was now the Chief Head of the Alabukum Company... yes, we have, yes, we did, and we have a chief head now, well a CEO in a listed company.*

At work, Afrika could not contain her excitement.

'Afrika, for one minute can you be quiet?' a colleague groaned.

'What do you mean, how can I be quiet, didn't you hear my news, that my sister has been appointed as the Chief Executive Director for the Alabakum Mining Company? Yes, CEO, truly!

'What?' Ronny inquired again.

'Yes, Sahara, the one I speak about, always, now CEO, you have to believe me, Ronny.'

'Oh, yes I heard the news. Is that your SAHARA?' Asked another colleague.

'Indeed, Sahara, my friend. Actually, my sister. We found out recently that we share the same... father, yes! It does not matter to us; we are very close, have always been. But that is not the same with the people who had sex... their problem?' Afrika blurted.

Back home, Johnny, Sahara's husband refused to admit the news of the appointment at first. 'How could she?' He had questioned. *It was not the norm from this community. Could it become a norm? We can become the norm.* He thought.

Meanwhile, Afrika was busy organising a celebratory party for Sahara, with friends and colleagues, following her appointment.

'Mumene and Veronique, we have to celebrate Sahara, together. You must come.' Afrika told them over the phone.

The celebratory night finally arrived. There was merriment everywhere. Everyone was ecstatic.

'Attention, Attention.' Mumene called. 'Ahbotta wants to make a toast.'

'Welcome everyone, please raise your glasses. A toast to my beautiful Sahara, for not only giving me four beautiful grandchildren, but for making us all proud. Congratulations on your appointment as the new Chief Executive Director. Johnny, I thank you for my Sahara. CHEERS to SAHARA. For good health and good leadership.'

'Cheers, Sahara, for Piercing the Thatch Ceiling;' came the response, while the clicking sound of glasses filled the room.

At that moment, Sahara, Veronique, Mumene and Afrika confirmed that their dream of life abroad was very much alive. They all had good jobs; Ahbotta, was happy, always ready to lend a hand; Johnny, the loving son, father and husband remained the sturdy rock; and both sets of twins got admission into private schools. The journey had just begun.

Author's Biography

A/Prof (Dr.) Watts has extensive experience and well-developed skills in governance and management and recognised for her strategic engagement capabilities, nationally and internationally. She is a strategic thinker, advocate, a public speaker and a Public Health Expert and a leader in women's health, gender health and international health. Dr Watts is an Academic at Federation University, Australia. She is also an associate in the School of Public Health and Preventive Medicine at Monash University, Australia. Dr Watts led VMware's strategic engagement for the Virtualize Africa Initiative, 'Cloud Computing' as the Academic Lead Consultant for Africa. This led to MOUs/ partnerships between VMware and the African Union Commission, and with Universities across

Africa for this Virtualize Africa Initiative. Dr Watts was recently recognised as a VMware Ambassador for her work on this Initiative. VMware is a multi-billion-dollar Silicon Valley based company. Dr Watts is on the Editorial /Advisory Boards of the East African Journal of Health sciences; and the WAGEDI-GUU International Journal for Sustainable Development. She was recognised with a Multicultural Award for Excellence by the Victorian Multicultural Commission & the Victorian State Government for her service in the Multiculturalism. The African Communities (Africa Day Australia) awarded her leadership and service to the communities.

As an academic at Victoria University for eleven years, she developed and led the Bachelor of Health Science in the College of Health and Biomedicine. She is an Honorary A/Prof in Public Health at Mekelle University in Ethiopia. Her expertise includes women's health, social inclusion, chronic disease prevention and management, health promotion, migrant and refugee health, strategic planning and health policy as well as curriculum development and teaching research methods.

Indeed, migration and migrant health needs have formed a significant part of Dr Watts's research expertise and she has published in refereed academic journals as well as being a reviewer and editor in public health related journals. She has participated in many International conferences and summits including the Gender Pre- Submit on Gender by the African Union; Improving health needs for women, increasing education opportunities particularly for girls and disadvantaged persons are key areas of interest for Dr Watts. Dr Watts born in Cameroon, started her career in Australia as a Registered Nurse, arriving here as a skilled migrant before moving on to Academic and other Leadership roles.

Dr Watts was appointed by the Department of Health to the reference group responsible for the implementation of the first Victorian Sexual and Reproductive Health Plan for the state. She served on the Federal Government Reference Group for the FGM Prevention Plan. Dr Watts served as a Commissioner with the Victorian Multicultural Commission; Board of Directors at Women's Health West (Deputy Chair for two years), a former Board Director at Western Health and currently serves on the Board of AMES Australia. Dr Watts Chairs the Australian African Academic Network. She is a Member of the African Science & Innovation Council with the African Union. She is the convenor of the African Diaspora Women Summit. Dr Watts is a respected public speaker, strategic thinker, communicator, and academic with local and global networks. Dr Watts is the author of *'SAHARA, piercing the Thatch Ceiling',* an intersectionality book that focuses on gender, culture and migrant women's journeys.

Book Summary

'*Sahara, Piercing the Thatch Ceiling*' narrates the story and journey of Sahara, a composite character through an intersectional gender lens. It is an inter-cultural, African, intergen-erational, migrant, refugee and an Australian story. The characters in this book have to navigate trials and obstacles experienced across the whole spectrum of the African diaspora from skilled migrants to refugees. Yet it is a story of ultimate triumph, thanks to the collective power of this group of women, the strength of their relationships, the will to persist through any hardship, and the determination to succeed. Cultural elements are woven through the stories in a way that gleans understanding while letting the narrative flow. In the human weaknesses and strengths that it reveals, Sahara and her friends and other characters in the book embrace the migrant dream. ***Mimmie C. N. C. Watts, Author.***

Photo @ the School of Public Health, Harvard University, Boston, USA.

Photo Credits: Mimmie Watts

www.ingramcontent.com/pod-product-compliance
Lightning Source LLC
Chambersburg PA
CBHW071058250626
47159CB00002B/511